A Merry Little Christmas

By

USA TODAY Bestselling Author

Denise Devine

A Sweet Christmas Romance

It's a merry little tale!

Denise Devine

A Merry Little Christmas

Print Edition

Copyright 2016 by Denise Devine

www.deniseannettedevine.com

ISBN: 978-0-9915956-8-6

Published in the United States of America

Cover Design by Anissa Turpin and Raine English

As always, to my critique group, the girls who just want to write fun!

~*~

Want to stay in touch with me? Sign up for my newsletter at http://eepurl.com/csOJZL and received a free romantic suspense short story. You'll be the first to know about my new releases, sales and special events.

Chapter 1

November 28th

Merry Connor's hand shook as she sat in her gold Cavalier and inserted the key into the ignition. Large snowflakes dropped onto the windshield, but the bleak November weather had little to do with her discomfort.

She turned the key.

Click—click—click—click—click.

"Come on, Rocket. Don't fail me now. I have ten minutes to get to work. Please, start!"

She didn't know where that noise came from under the hood, but it definitely sounded like trouble. Whispering a short prayer, she took a deep breath and tried again. This time she heard nothing but the sound of her own heartbeat pounding in her ears.

Rocket, the name her nine-year-old son labeled the car when she first brought it home, had been a reliable vehicle until now. However, from the looks of things, Rocket's next trip would amount to a ride to the garage on the back of a tow truck. Unfortunately, towing didn't come cheap. Neither did car repairs. For a divorced mother of two who could barely make ends meet, taking on more debt four weeks before Christmas meant financial disaster. She didn't even have a Christmas tree yet, but that idea looked doubtful now.

Merry heaved a loud sigh and tipped her head back against the cold headrest. "Why is this happening to me? Don't I have enough problems already?"

Her phone began to ring a familiar tune in her purse. Speaking of problems... She squared her shoulders, willing herself to remain calm as she reluctantly fished it out and pressed the speaker button. "Hi, Mom."

"What's the matter?" Lauren Benson asked sharply. "You sound upset."

"No... I'm fine." Merry grabbed her tote bag and shoved open the car door, not in the mood for her mother's daily lecture on fiscal responsibility. "I'm on my way to work."

"You're starting rather early today, aren't you? What about the kids?"

"I've already dropped them off at school." She shut the car door and started walking down the driveway. The huge, feathery snowflakes were falling faster, covering everything with a fluffy layer of white. She would have been at work right now enjoying a rich cup of coffee with her coworkers if she hadn't forgotten at home the apron containing her pens, wine key, crumber and other items needed for her serving job at the Nicollet Island Inn. "I'm working longer hours now. One of the servers turned in her notice and my manager offered me the shift. Instead of making the first cut at twelve-thirty, I'm now coming in a half-hour earlier and staying on until three o'clock, when the dinner shift starts. The kids don't get out of school until four so I'll have enough time to check out and drive over there to pick them up."

That is, once she'd solved her car problems. Today she'd have to walk to Marcy-Holmes Elementary School to get the kids.

At the end of the driveway, she turned right onto Nicollet Street and picked up the pace. According to her phone, she had exactly eight minutes to travel three-and-a-half blocks to the Nicollet Island Inn and clock in for work. Luckily, the blocks were short and she always wore non-slip shoes.

"Have you started Christmas shopping yet?" Lauren asked. "I thought you and the kids might like to meet Dad and me at Rosedale Mall on Saturday for lunch. Cody and Lily could get their pictures taken with Santa."

If only...

"Actually, Mom, I have to work a double shift that day." Her heart ached knowing she had to miss such a special moment with her kids, but she couldn't help it—especially now with her car on the fritz. "My manager had to pull several servers from the dining room to staff Christmas parties in the banquet rooms. I really need the money, so I was wondering if you and Dad could watch the kids for me. My heat bill came yesterday and I wasn't counting on it being so high."

"I suppose," Lauren said, stretching out the word "suppose" to let Merry know of her disapproval of her daughter's last-minute schedule change. "We'll pick up the kids early on Saturday and keep them overnight. I hate getting them up when you come to take them home. Lily gets so cranky when she's awakened from a sound sleep." She paused for a moment. "You should sell that creaky old house and move into a nice townhome. I see dozens of affordable properties in Minneapolis listed for sale every week in the Sunday paper. Some are right in the Marcey-Holmes area. The kids wouldn't even have to change schools."

Merry's jaw clenched at the mention of the word *affordable*. The deliberate, calculated actions of her husband before their divorce had ruined her credit, making it impossible to get a loan for anything, including a decent car. She'd obtained her present home only through a sheer stroke of luck—and the personal recommendation of a good friend who knew of her unfortunate situation. Buying a *nice* townhouse meant asking her parents for help, something she'd determined to stop doing as soon as she could. Working a longer shift took her a step closer to that goal and one day she wouldn't have to rely on them at all. Until then...

"Mom, I don't want a townhouse. I like it here on Nicollet Island. Even though it's in the center of the city, the island has a small town feel and I love my neighbors."

At Grove Street, she turned left, heading for East Island Avenue.

"Merry, it's smack dab in the middle of the Mississippi River for crying out loud! I worry every day about Cody and Lily playing in the park. What if they went down to the water's edge and fell in?"

"I never let them go to the park without me. I don't allow them to leave our block much less go all the way to the other end of the island by themselves."

"Why won't you at least consider it? You know it would be safer for the kids. Besides, you wouldn't have to shovel the sidewalk or mow the yard and the utilities wouldn't be such a burden on your finances."

Merry reached East Island Avenue and saw the historic Nicollet Island Inn, a square, three-story limestone building with aqua trim. She glanced at her phone and began to power walk. "I'd have a living room the size of a postage stamp and the kids wouldn't have anywhere to play," she said between deep breaths. "Mom, I know my house needs a lot of work, but it has character and a nice yard. I'll get it fixed up someday."

After I get my car repaired and buy a Christmas tree and pay the heat bill...

She hustled past De La Salle High School and crossed the Inn's rear parking lot, listening to her mother go over the plan for Saturday. "Sounds great, Mom. Gotta go. I need to clock in and get to work," she said, breathless. "Thanks for taking the kids. They're going to have a lot of fun. Oh, and say hi to Dad. Bye."

She shoved her phone into her pocket and pushed open the Inn's back door. Sounds of a busy commercial kitchen diverted her attention, giving her a temporary respite from her problems. She waved to the chef on duty as he called out an order to one of his line cooks. A server asked for a side of toast while pulling an array of completed dishes from under the heating lights and arranging them on a large tray. Kitchen workers stood at their stations, chopping vegetables for soup and preparing items for the dishes of the day.

Merry hastened to find her security card and swiped one of the computers at the server station, clocking in exactly on time. She hung her empty tote and jacket on a hook then tied her long, black apron around her waist, mentally preparing herself for a busy day with friendly, interesting customers and great tips.

Though she was barely making it financially, life was good compared to two years ago when she'd lost everything—thanks to her lying, deceiving ex-husband. She'd come a long way since then and didn't intend to look back. Even so, it would be a long time before she'd trust anyone with her heart again.

Maybe *never*.

****

Anthony Lewis sat at a table at Sam's Bar, surrounded by multi-colored Christmas lights and the woodsy aroma of pine as he stared at his brother-in-law in disbelief. "You want me to...*what?*"

Wearing a gray ski sweater that matched the premature aging streaks in his black hair, Neal Carter leaned forward and looked him in the eye. "You heard what I said, Tony," Neal replied, addressing him by his nickname. "I want you to get friendly with the wife of the employee who embezzled money from me and convince her to confide in you where he has it hidden."

Tony cleared his throat and glanced around, hoping no one had overheard Neal's request. "Are you serious?"

"More than you know."

The man sounded so ridiculous Tony didn't know whether to laugh in his face or change the subject. "You're crazy," he said, settling on the direct approach. "That's impossible and you know it."

Neal pushed his empty beer glass aside and clasped his hands on the table, his green eyes widening with excitement. "Actually, it's perfect." He tapped his fingers on the table to the music echoing throughout the room as Frank Sinatra and his female chorus sang about j-i-n-g-l-e bells. "I've got it all planned out. It'll work, believe me."

Tony shook his head. "I don't care what you've got up your sleeve; I'm not going to wine and dine some chick to get her into bed for the sole purpose of extracting a midnight confession for you. Find somebody else. I'm not your delivery boy."

"I'm not suggesting you wine and dine and sleep with anyone." Neal frowned. "I don't care how you get the information out of her. I just want you to find out where Aidan Connor hid the money so I can get my million dollars back. There's a ten percent finders fee in this deal for recovering it. Just think what you could do with an extra hundred grand in your pocket."

"I don't need your money."

Neal lifted one brow. "Everybody needs more money. Including you."

He's not going to let this go until I either agree to it or tell him off...

10

"Why me?" Tony snapped, becoming irritated. "Why don't you hire a private detective to do your dirty work?"

"I did. Paid him good money to find out what the woman knows, but so far, he hasn't delivered any useful information. It's time to change tactics." Neal signaled the cocktail server for another round. Sinatra's song ended and the music switched to an instrumental rendition of "I'll be Home for Christmas."

Tony raised his hand to get the girl's attention. "Excuse me," he said to the tall brunette wearing jeans and a shiny gold blouse as she stood at the bar, arranging drinks on a tray. Behind her, a dozen red and white fuzzy Christmas stockings hung on a string along the cedar-paneled wall. "Cancel the beer for me. I'll take a Coke." He turned back to Neal. "Why are you so set on pressuring me into this?"

Neal went silent for a moment. "Because you're the only one I trust."

The manager suddenly appeared at their table with their lunch order and set the heavy platters on the table. "Is there anything else I can get for you?"

"We're good," Neal said as he sized up his food. "Thanks."

The pungent aroma of fresh grilled beef and thick, crispy fries made Tony's stomach growl. He reached for the ketchup, squirted a large puddle on his plate then dipped his burger into the thick red sauce and took a huge bite.

"Sorry I got so testy," Neal said once they were alone again. "You're right. This isn't about the money. Our insurance carrier settled with Faith and me a while back. It's the principle of the thing." He pulled the upper half of the bun off his burger, dumped a garnish of coleslaw on the meat then placed the bun back on top, pressing it down. "Aidan Connor worked as our accountant for ten years. We had no idea he was siphoning money out of the store's account right under our noses. He was smart; a little here, a little there. Our liquor sales run at such a high volume we never missed it."

The server dropped off their drinks. "How's everything?"

They both nodded to signal they were satisfied and continued to munch on their meals.

Tony reached for his Coke. "What makes you think he still has the money? Most embezzlers spend it as fast as they get it."

Neal set down his burger. "Aidan is cheap. He doesn't—I mean *didn't*—fish, hunt, gamble or buy expensive toys. He lived in a modest home and didn't believe in buying a brand new car because they depreciated so fast. The police investigation didn't turn up any international activity or unusually large accounts established in his kids' names." Neal picked up a French fry and swirled it in a glob of ketchup on his plate. His hand stopped in mid-air, pointing the fry at Tony. "Make no mistake; he's got that cash squirreled away somewhere. I don't know if he's converted it to silver or gold or maybe it's still in currency, but I'll bet you anything, he and the missus are planning to make a run for it with their booty as soon as he gets out of prison."

Tony set down his Coke. "If the guy was so smart, how did you catch him?"

"When we expanded the store our business nearly doubled and we had to hire more people, including a second accountant. She's the one who eventually caught on to him." Neal's jaw clenched. "Otherwise, he'd still be ripping us off."

So full he couldn't eat another bite, Tony sat back and exhaled a large sigh. "I understand how you feel, Neal, but I don't know anything about undercover work. I'm a real estate investor. I have no idea how to approach Aidan Connor's wife and, frankly, I don't want to know."

"Don't worry about it. You're good at dealing with people." Neal wiped his hands on his napkin then reached under the table and grabbed a file from his briefcase. "Her name is Merry Connor, that's M-e-r-r-y, and she lives in a house on Nicollet Island."

"There you go," Tony said, finding the ammunition to shut down his brother-in-law's ridiculous idea. He knew that area like the back of his hand. "All of the houses on Nicollet Island are designated historic. The entire island is historic, for that matter. She must have used a nice chunk of the money to acquire a property there."

"No, she didn't." Neal pushed his plate aside and set the manila folder on the table. "The house she bought was owned by a woman who'd lived in it for sixty years. The husband passed away about twenty years ago and the wife became a recluse. When the old lady died, she left the property to her favorite niece and nephew. They didn't want to sink any money into the place to bring it up to code so they sold it 'as is' on a contract-for-deed to Merry. This is where you come in." Neal flashed a smug grin. "You're going to buy that contract and use it as an excuse to introduce yourself to her."

"What?" Tony started, almost knocking over his Coke. "You're out of your mind. I'm not donating to this ridiculous cause." He stood up to leave. "You stick to your business, Neal, and I'll stick to mine. I don't buy anything until I've thoroughly checked it out and determined it's worth adding to my portfolio."

Neal flipped open the folder and shuffled through the papers as though he hadn't heard a word. "I spoke to Gerald Grange; he's the administrator of the old lady's estate and one of the contract holders. He's anxious to dump it because he's trying to expand his consulting business and needs the money." Neal waved his hand to indicate he didn't know the whole story and cared less. "Anyway, he wants to cash out." Neal held out a copy of the contract for Tony to examine. "If you can come up with the funds by the end of this week, he's willing to discount it twenty-five percent."

Tony glanced down and saw the contract amount. *The house*

must be a total wreck to let it go that cheap.

He dropped the contract on the table. "Not interested. Thanks for lunch."

"Wait." Neal reached out, grabbing Tony by the arm. "I didn't want to bring this up, but you owe it to Faith to give my idea a chance. She deserves justice for what Aidan did to her."

"Justice my—" Tony shook off Neal's hand and leaned over the table, face-to-face with his brother-in-law. "Don't even think of dragging my sister into your little game of revenge."

"She's already involved whether you like it or not. Aidan stole the money from *both* of us." Neal glared at him. "I see you've conveniently forgotten how Faith came through for you when you needed *her*. As I recall, she drove you to the hospital to identify Cherie and Evan's bodies then took over the funeral arrangements because you were so distraught. She wanted to spare you the trauma of planning the burial of your own wife and son. Is this how you repay her?"

Neal's low blow angered Tony, but even worse, it triggered a fresh wave of grief as the chilling memory of that snowy December night and the images of his lifeless wife and child flashed through his mind. Over time, he'd convinced himself he'd made progress in dealing with their deaths. Neal's thoughtless words proved otherwise. Though the accident happened nearly three years ago, the pain of losing the greatest love of his life and his precious child still throbbed like a fresh wound, leaving a gaping hole in his soul.

"Don't ever bring up that night again," he said shakily, bracing his hands on the table, "or so help me, I'll—"

Neal pushed his chair back and countered with a sheepish laugh. "Okay, okay, I'll admit my situation isn't as life altering as what happened to you, but nevertheless, this business with Aidan Connor is destroying my marriage. His thievery broke Faith's heart. Aidan Connor was more than an employee. He was a longtime friend, someone she'd known since high school. His betrayal still fuels her depression because it has shaken her trust in people, including *me*."

The mention of his sister's mental state caused Tony to pause. He knew she'd been dealing with depression for a long time, and during the holidays, it always seemed to get worse. He couldn't deny that she'd helped him through the darkest time of his life, but it ticked him off to hear Neal play the guilt card to coerce him into action.

He grabbed his jacket and slid his arms into it. "Does she know you're orchestrating this little mission-impossible on her behalf?"

"Of course not," Neal said, "and she's not going to know about it until I get the money back. I want to give her some good news, not an empty promise."

Tony gripped his hips with his hands. "This is such a long shot I wouldn't know where to start."

Neal's face brightened. "You can start by buying Merry's contract and making friends with her. You two have a lot in common. She's about ten years younger than Aidan. That puts her close to your age—middle thirties, right? She's lost her spouse; she has small children and owns a house, so obviously she likes real estate."

Tony stared at Neal in frustration. *Yeah, that makes no sense. How many drinks did you have before I got here, anyway?* He sighed, feeling torn. "*If* I decide to do this, I'll do it on my terms."

Neal stood. "All right, what are your terms?"

"You get *one shot* at this and I make no promises, so don't get your hopes up. I'll set up a meeting with her to go over the contract and if I learn something useful through the course of our conversation, I'll let you know. There's no 'Plan B,' no further argument from you. I want no part of whatever scheme you're concocting against this woman. Is that understood? As far as I'm concerned, this is a business deal and nothing more."

15

"Understood." Neal signaled to the server to bring his tab as Elvis crooned "Blue Christmas." He cut a hard glance at Tony. "While you're thinking this over I want you to do something for me. Try to visualize the face of Aidan Conner after he gets out of prison and he realizes we've found his hidey-hole because his stash is gone." His eyes narrowed. "And that his time served gained him absolutely *nothing*."

Chapter 2

December 4th

Merry surveyed the dirty dishes strewn about her kitchen, wishing she hadn't let Cody and Lily talk her into baking chocolate chip cookies from scratch. The kids had been eager to help and miraculously, they'd managed not to burn any, but it had taken all morning to make one batch. She snatched the bags of flour and sugar off the counter, eager to get everything back in order before her one o'clock appointment with Anthony Lewis.

She opened a cabinet and took out an empty plastic ice cream pail. "Cody," Merry said, turning around, "we've got company coming in about an hour so please go upstairs and clean your room. Take Lily with you. Lily, I want you to gather up the books on your bed. Put them all back in the bookcase."

Cody sat at the table, shaking his head, his bullish expression conveying the stubborn streak she'd been dealing with since the divorce. "I don't want to clean my room."

"I don't want to clean my room..." Lily said, parroting him. Lately, everything Cody said came out of Lily's mouth as an instant replay.

Merry pulled the cover off the container and began filling it with the cookies that she'd stacked in rows on a sheet of waxed paper. "The house is a mess and our company will be here soon so I need you both to do your part."

Cody's sandy curls bounced as his head bobbed up. "Are they bringing pizza?"

Lily reached for a cookie. "Is Grandma coming over to our house, Momma?" She sighed dramatically. "Do you have to go to work *again*?"

"Grandma's staying home today. I don't work on Sunday." Merry snatched the cookie from her six-year-old daughter and dropped it in the pail. "No more sweets until your rooms are clean."

Cody gave her a curious look. "Who's coming over then?"

"A man is stopping by to view the house and discuss the contract with me." Merry noted his confused look and hoped it didn't give way to a string of questions she didn't have time to answer. She pretended not to see his expression and scooped up the cookies, filling the pail as fast as she could. The sooner she got them packed and out of the way, the sooner she could usher the kids upstairs to get their chores done. She closed the lid and set the container on the only clean spot on the kitchen counter. "All done," she announced as she crushed the waxed paper into a ball and shoved it into the trash. "Now get going, you two, or there will be no television tonight."

"Aw right..." Cody grumbled.

It saddened her to threaten to take away privileges, but sometimes it was the only way to get Cody to cooperate. He turned and stomped out of the kitchen. Lily followed behind her older brother; her long blonde curls flouncing as she mimicked his footsteps through the house.

Getting down to business, Merry worked speedily putting away the baking powder and other items while filling the sink with soapy water. Her dishwasher, an avocado model dating back to the 70s, didn't have a scratch on it, but it didn't work, either. Given its age, she saw no point in fixing it. Nevertheless, she couldn't afford to buy a new one. She didn't mind washing dishes by hand, but with two kids, she always had a sink full of dirty plates and cups.

Merry checked the time again, noting she only had fifty minutes now to put the house in order and inspect the kids' rooms. She had no idea what this investor, Anthony Lewis, wanted to discuss with her, nor did she understand why Gerald Grange had sold her contract to him. She'd always paid her house payment on time, sometimes at the expense of something else equally as important. Glancing out the kitchen window, she stared wistfully at her gold Cavalier. Covered with several inches of new snow, it looked like an over-sized Christmas ornament. She didn't know how she'd manage without transportation, but the car had to wait its turn. Which might take a while...

I wonder why Anthony Lewis wants to meet me in person, Merry thought as she scrubbed the large green Tupperware bowl she'd used to make the cookie dough. *I don't mind showing him the house, but I hope we can focus on business issues and not my past. Aidan and I are divorced. I have nothing to do with him and nothing to say about him anymore. Period.*

She'd spent the last two years dodging embarrassing questions from friends, relatives and bill collectors who were curious about Aidan's arrest and imprisonment. Friends and family were sympathetic of her dire situation. The bill collectors were not. She hated the one question most people asked her. Everyone wanted to know what happened to all the money Aidan embezzled.

*So do I...*she thought desperately.

She had nothing to do with either the crime or the missing

money, but many people suspected her of collaborating with Aidan to hide it—including the local authorities. She wished she could find the stolen cash and give it back because most of all, she wanted to clear her name.

The front doorbell caught her by surprise at 12:45 pm.

"He's early," Merry complained with a sigh as she walked through the house. She hadn't accomplished as much as she'd planned, but at least she'd managed to clean up the kitchen and sweep cookie crumbs off the floor.

She brushed flour off her white sweater and skinny jeans as she walked into the living room and peered through the leaded glass window in the front door. A tall man, mid-thirties with wavy, dark hair waited on her front porch holding a manila folder. He wore a dark *Under Armour* hoodie, unzipped, a navy knit shirt and khakis. She stared at him in surprise, anticipating someone much different. Gerald Grange had described him as an experienced investor owning dozens of properties and contracts-for-deed, giving her the expectation of a wizened, gray-haired man wearing a business suit and carrying a briefcase. Anthony Lewis' casual look showing off his broad shoulders, muscular chest and arms made him look more like someone's personal trainer than a seasoned businessman.

She opened the door as far as the chain would allow and peered at him through the narrow opening. "Hello."

His intense blue eyes held hers. "Merry Connor?" At her response, he nodded curtly and held out a business card. "I'm Anthony Lewis."

Merry perused the card then closed the door and slid back the chain to open it all the way. "I'm pleased to meet you, Mr. Lewis." She shook his outstretched hand. The strong, yet gentle grip of his fingers startled her, causing her breath to catch in her throat.

She moved aside for him to enter. "Please, come in, Mr.

Lewis."

"Just call me Tony," he said in a businesslike tone as he crossed the threshold.

"Someone's here!" Cody's shout echoed throughout the upper level. Thundering footsteps sounded overhead. The kids appeared at the top of the stairs and charged down the staircase like stampeding buffalo.

Cody stopped at the second stair from the bottom. He'd changed into a green and black camouflage print T-shirt and black cargo pants. He catapulted off the stair, landing both feet on the floor with a loud thud. "Did you come to talk to my mom about the contract?"

Lily followed her brother, repeating the question and leaping off the step before Merry could stop her. Luckily, she caught Lily before the child slipped on the smooth oak floor and landed on her backside, averting an embarrassing scene of tears and loud wailing. Lily smiled up at Tony, revealing a gap where her front baby teeth used to be. A small, uneven patch of white jutted out where one new tooth emerged. "What's your name? I'm Lily!"

"Settle down, you two." Merry turned to Tony, exasperated that her children were showing off for their visitor. "Sorry about all the commotion. The kids always get excited when we get company."

Tony gazed down at Lily with an amused grin. "Hello there, Miss Lily. I'm Tony."

Lily gave him a toothless smile and pointed to the glittery Disney character on the front of her light blue shirt. "I like Elsa. Who do you like, Elsa or Anna?"

Tony's smile faded as he stared down at Lily, perplexed. "*Who*?"

Merry laughed and slid her arm around Cody, ruffling her son's curly mop of sandy hair. "This is Cody," she said, changing the subject.

"He's nine."

Cody shied away. "Mom, *don't* mess up my hair. I'm not a baby anymore."

"And this is Lily," Merry said, dropping a quick kiss on the top of her daughter's blonde head. "She *is* my baby. Lily's six."

"I'm in first grade." Lily tugged on Tony's sleeve, the fine curve of her golden brows knit together. "What's a contract?"

Tony opened the folder and showed Lily the document. "It's a legal agreement between me and your mom."

Lily stared at the printed pages and shrugged. "I like coloring books."

Merry opened the front closet. "Tony, may I take your jacket?"

After she put Tony's hoodie away, she took Lily by the hand. "Let's go into the kitchen."

"You have a beautiful place here," Tony remarked as they passed through the dining room. "The interior looks remarkably well preserved."

"I fell in love with this house the moment I saw it." Merry slowed her pace in the dining room. "This room is my favorite spot. The dark woodwork and the built-in, mirrored buffet make it special to me because it's a wonderful area for entertaining. Unfortunately, I don't get much chance to use it."

Once they reached the kitchen, she pulled out a chair at the table. "Have a seat." She walked over to the sink and leaned against the counter, folding her arms. "I've loved this house since the first time I saw it. I never want to move."

So if you've come to buy me out, I'm not selling...

He remained standing as his gaze swept the room, taking in her outdated kitchen with "avocado" green appliances and Formica butcher-block countertops as though looking for something in particular. What did he want?

He set his folder on the table. "Something in this kitchen smells wonderful."

"We made cookies!" Cody pointed toward the ice cream pail. "Do you want one?"

"Not now, Cody," Merry scolded. "We're talking—"

Lily saw Cody dash toward the counter and chased after him. "I want to give him one! Let *me* do it!"

Merry moved toward the pail, reaching for it. "Cody, I said—"

Lily and Cody grabbed the pail at the same time. They pulled so hard the flimsy metal handle came apart and the pail slipped from their hands, dropping to their feet with a loud crash. The impact blew the lid off and cookies exploded throughout the kitchen, rolling all over the floor.

"Lily! Cody!" Merry threw her hands in the air, livid with frustration. "Pick up every last one of those cookies *right now*! And throw them in the garbage."

Lily retrieved one off the floor and held it out to Tony, her soft brown eyes filling with tears. "I just wanted to give you one, that's all."

"Thank you." Tony laughed and accepted the cookie. "Don't cry. It looks okay to me. We'll just apply the five second rule." He took a large bite. "Mmmm... This is good. I haven't eaten a homemade chocolate chip cookie in years."

She picked a second cookie off the floor. "Do you want another one?"

He perused her with an amused grin. "You're quite the little cutie, aren't you?"

"Throw it away, Lily. It's dirty." Merry replaced the lid on the few remaining cookies in the pail then set it on a high shelf in the cabinet and shut the door. *So long to that batch,* she thought. She pulled a white plastic garbage can from under the sink and quickly helped the kids dispose of the cookies on the floor. Once they'd completed that task she put the garbage can away and said, "Now, you two go upstairs and finish cleaning your rooms. When you're done you can have one more treat, but not until I say so."

Cody perked up. "We can? Okay!" He raced out of the room with Lily trailing behind.

Merry went back to her place against the counter. "I apologize for all the fuss. My kids haven't been the same since my divorce. All of the turmoil we've gone through in the last two years has been hard on them, especially Cody."

"It doesn't bother me." Tony sat at the table and opened his folder. "My son used to..." He went still as the sentence trailed off.

"Oh, you have a son, too?"

"I, ah..." His sudden, guarded expression caught her by surprise, giving her an uncomfortable feeling that she'd said something wrong. "Let's talk about the contract," he said, redirecting the subject back to the reason for his visit. "I'd like to go over the salient points with you to make sure we both have the same understanding of the terms."

"Okay..." Her muscles tensed as she waited for him to continue, wondering what brought on such an abrupt change.

"The conditions laid out are mostly in your favor," he said, scanning the pages. "It's as though the Granges were looking out for *your* interests rather than their own."

"Why do you say that?"

"Your down payment was waived and the taxes and insurance were covered by the seller for the first year." He looked up. "That's amazing. How did you manage that?"

"The Granges are close friends of mine. Well, Suzanne is. She's Gerald's sister. I lived next door to her grandmother most of my life and saw Suzanne almost every weekend. When her great-aunt died and left the house to her and her brother, she convinced Gerald to sell it to me."

Tony paused, scanning another page. "There's no penalty for late payments and you can miss up to three before you default." He gave her a pointed look. "Are your installments ever late?"

"Nope." She glared at him. *How nice of you to ask...*

He continued reading. "The contract states that you must refinance after five years, but if you can't find a lending institution to give you a loan, you have the option to renegotiate this agreement." He drew in a deep breath, as if regretting the acquisition of this deal. "What would preclude you from refinancing?"

"I guess it would depend on the inspection report. This house needs a lot of work to bring it up to code."

He sat back in his chair and gazed around the room. "What exactly needs fixing?"

"I need insulation in the attic, a new hot water heater and energy efficient windows for a start," Merry replied, ticking off the items on her fingers. "The plumbing leaks, my toilet won't quit running, I need to have the kitchen wiring updated and the appliances are older than I am. The floors need refinishing, the bedrooms have shag carpeting from the 70s and—"

Tony held up his palms. "Okay, okay, I get it." He flipped the manila folder shut. "The Granges gave you a very favorable interest rate. One percent over the commercial lending rate is excellent for a person in your position."

This guy had a lot of nerve. "And what position would that be?"

He shoved the folder aside and turned toward her. "I've

25

reviewed your credit report. You've had some problems in the past."

Here it comes...

Merry braced herself against the counter with both hands. "That wasn't my fault."

He didn't answer, but the skepticism in his deep blue eyes silently said, "*Are you kidding me?*"

"Look," she said, her knuckles turning white from gripping the counter so hard, "my ex-husband worked as an accountant when we were married and he insisted on handling all of our funds. I didn't know he wasn't paying the bills, and by the time I found out, our financial situation had passed the point of no return."

"What did he do with the money," Tony asked abruptly.

"I have *no* idea."

He gave her a skeptical look.

He has no right to judge me, but then, he's no different from anyone else who's heard the story...

"I know it sounds like a convenient excuse," Merry said, pushing away from the counter, "but I'm just as much a victim as the people whose money Aidan embezzled."

"I didn't say your husband embezzled money from anyone."

She placed her hands on her hips. "No, but you know he did. You, along with everyone else in this town, saw his mug shot plastered on the nightly news for weeks." She cringed inwardly at the thought of her kids hearing negative things about their father. It made her even angrier with Aidan for subjecting his children to such humiliation and shame. "Aidan took out a second mortgage on our house without my knowledge and drained every account we had. Was I upset? Of course, I was! I trusted him, but obviously, he didn't trust me, or care about the welfare of his family. When I confronted him, he said he didn't have the money and refused to talk about it again."

Her mind flashed back to that day and the cold stare in Aidan's gray eyes, the indifference in his voice, as though she had no business asking, but she brushed it aside and kept on. "My creditors didn't care about our welfare, either. They repossessed everything we owned, leaving me broke and homeless—with two children to feed. My parents took us in until I could get a job and a secondhand car. Then Suzanne Grange approached me about buying this house and said she'd convinced her brother to sell it to me on terms I could afford. I had the chance to start all over again and I jumped into it with both feet. I'm as poor as a church mouse, but this time I'm controlling *my own* destiny." Her voice shook so much she could hardly talk. "I'll probably never find the money Aidan stole, but if I did, I'd give it back to clear my name."

Her cell phone suddenly rang.

With an unsteady hand, Merry picked it off the counter and looked at the screen. "Someone from my job is calling. Excuse me, I have to take this."

She hurried out of the kitchen, disappointed in herself for doing the one thing she'd vowed not to do—repeating the story of her husband's duplicity one more time...

****

Tony shoved back his chair and jumped to his feet. "Merry, I'm sorry. I didn't mean—"

His words echoed through an empty room. She'd already fled the kitchen, her long blonde hair flowing behind her as she left him standing alone. He stared at the doorway she'd disappeared through, mulling over her outburst.

Either she is one talented actress or her anger is real.

His instincts were leaning toward the second point. He didn't know where Neal had obtained his information, but his brother-in-law had Merry Connor all wrong. For someone who supposedly conspired with her husband, guarding the stolen goods until he got out of prison, she certainly didn't act like it. Her flushed cheeks, rigid stance and trembling voice appeared to be genuine. Her story, if true, must have been a nightmare to endure.

How could Aidan Connor do that to her? Why would he deliberately sabotage the future of his own children and his wife?

They'd covered everything he wanted to discuss, including the subject of Merry's credit. Her business call sounded urgent, so he decided to take his leave. He cast a cursory look around her kitchen once more then headed for the front closet to retrieve his jacket. The sparse furnishings were secondhand. The entire house looked mismatched, as though Merry had decorated with garage sale bargains. The woman didn't own a single item of value as far as he could tell— not even a decent television. She definitely didn't live like a woman who had at least a million bucks stashed away.

Cody came bouncing down the stairs, meeting him at the front door. "Who called?

"Who called?" Lily repeated as she followed behind her brother, crashing into his back on the bottom step. "Are Grandma and Grandpa coming over?"

"I don't know. You'll have to ask your mom about that." Tony smiled to himself. These kids were quite a handful, but at the same time, they made an endearing pair. He wondered, wistfully, if his own son would exude as much energy if he were alive.

"I'm hungry," Cody said and rubbed his stomach. "I wish we were having pizza for supper."

Lily pushed past her brother. "Tony, are you eating at our house tonight?"

"No, I'm afraid not." He pulled his jacket from the closet and slipped it on. The lonely, faraway expression on Cody's face made him pause. Fate had dealt the boy a raw deal, losing his father the way he did. Every boy needed a man's influence, someone to teach him values and guide him through the bumps and bruises of life. "Maybe some other time," he said slowly, wondering why guilt pressed on his heart from all sides.

He headed back to the kitchen to retrieve his folder, passing Merry in the dining room. She sat at the table, still talking with someone on the phone. He waved at her, politely letting her know he would let himself out.

In the kitchen, he reached for the folder and shoved it inside his jacket.

"Do you have a dog?"

"What?" Tony spun around at the sound of Lily's voice. This kid was an encyclopedia of questions. He found her staring at him intently with one hand on her hip and her head tipped to one side. "Why do you ask, Lily? Do you have one?"

With a deep sigh, she shook her head. "We used to, but my daddy gave it away. My momma said we don't have no money to buy food for another doggie."

The disappointment in her big brown eyes melted his heart. He knelt to meet her face to face. She looked so much like Merry and her expression was so sincere he couldn't help but smile. "Do you want a dog?"

Lily nodded vigorously.

Merry appeared at the kitchen doorway. "I apologize for making you wait so long. That was the scheduler at the Nicollet Island Inn. I work there as a server." She stared straight ahead, her brows creased.

He rose to his feet. "Is everything all right?"

"Yes, of course." She leaned against the door jam. "I volunteered to work Saturday night."

"Yeah," Cody blurted, "that's 'cause we gotta get the car fixed."

Merry looked down, pre-occupied with slipping the phone into her pocket, but he could plainly see the flush in her cheeks.

Tony zipped up his jacket. "How do you get around without a car?"

She looked up. "I manage," she said stiffly. "I take the bus to get groceries and usually get a ride from a coworker after my shift, but sometimes I walk." She shrugged. "The Inn is only three and a half blocks away and this is a quiet neighborhood."

The thought of Merry walking home alone after dark sent chills down Tony's spine. The route from the Inn to her house took her past the high school, over the Nicollet Street Bridge and a stretch of parkland. Tony stepped over to the window and observed her car covered with snow. "What's wrong with your Cavalier?"

"I wish I knew."

His mind churned with curiosity. "Mind if I take a look?"

Before she could reply, he threw open the back door and stepped outside, taking in the cool November sunshine. He brushed the snow off the front of the car with his sleeve and lifted the hood. "What happens when you start it up?"

Merry stood behind him, shivering as she shoved her arms into a lemon-colored sweater. "Nothing...it won't start."

He scoped out the different components that could cause a problem. The battery looked to be at least ten years old. The manufacturer of that brand had discontinued it a long time ago. "See this?" He pointed to the battery cables. "They're corroded. Why didn't

30

you replace them when you had the car winterized?"

She stepped closer and peered under the hood. "The garage I use wanted four hundred dollars to do the job. I didn't have the money so I just had the oil changed."

Tony turned his head, wondering where she took her car for maintenance, but the moment he gazed into her soft brown eyes he forgot what he wanted to say. "You...ah...h-had the oil changed. That—that's good..." Something inside him stirred and he couldn't look away.

Neither spoke for a moment.

"I should have done more," she said slowly as their gazes held. "I should have worked extra hours to get the car serviced."

Feeling awkward and self-conscious for no reason, he turned his attention back to the engine. "It might have developed problems anyway. I know of a reasonable repair shop not far from here where I take my car when it needs service. If you live within a mile, they'll tow your car into the shop at no charge. I can give you the number if you'd like it."

"That would be great, Tony. Thank you."

"I don't mean to criticize, but why didn't you park the car in the garage?"

"I can't." Merry lifted her hands, palms up, showing her frustration. "The garage door is broken."

He turned and stared at her in astonishment. "You're kidding."

"I wish I were. I told you this place needed a lot of work."

Tony shut the hood and walked over to the two-car garage. He tried the side door, found it unlocked and stepped inside, noting that at least one thing worked properly. Poking around, it didn't take him long to figure out the problem. He pressed the activation button and the garage door opener hummed, but nothing moved. He turned to Merry, who had trailed in behind him. "The rollers need replacing, that's all." His voice echoed through the empty building. "Get that fixed and you're good to go."

She responded with a skeptical laugh. "Yeah, well, when I win the lottery I'll be sure to get right on it."

Tony walked her to the back steps of the house, stopping there to say goodbye and go on his way. "It's been nice meeting you." He pulled a card from his billfold and offered it to her. "Here's the information on Carlson's Car Care. They're the best repair shop in this part of town and booked solid all the time so call them as soon as you can to get an appointment. If you have trouble getting a complimentary tow because your location is past the one-mile limit, let me know. I'll talk to the manager."

"Thank you, that's really nice of you. I appreciate the offer." Merry took the card. "I enjoyed meeting you, too."

If you were truly a nice guy, you'd fix it for her...

Startled by his own thoughts, he said farewell and headed for his Jeep, but as he walked to the curb, his desire to help her out wouldn't leave him alone. He mulled over a couple things he could try to get her Chevy running again and composed a mental list of the parts he needed. If his hunch proved correct, he'd have her car fixed in a day.

Walking down the driveway, he slowed his pace and pulled out his phone to make a call to Roberto's Pizza. The idea had been lurking in the back of his mind ever since he talked to Cody. "Yeah," he said to the teenager who answered, "I want to order a large pizza to be delivered to Nicollet Street. How long will it take?"

Tony placed the order and smiled to himself as he opened the door to his red Jeep. It would have been worth it to stick around just to see the happiness on the kids' faces, especially Cody's, when the deliveryman showed up with the pizza, but he didn't want to give Merry the opportunity to argue with him over the bill. Besides, he had other things to do.

First, he needed to stop into an auto parts store and get the parts for Merry's Cavalier then run over to the hardware store and buy replacement rollers for her garage door. After that, he planned to call Neal and give him an update on their agreement.

The deal was off.

Chapter 3

December 5th

"Why is the hood open on my car?" Merry craned her neck to identify the intruder as Suzanne Grange stopped her SUV on Nicollet Street in front of Merry's yellow, two-story house. "Who is messing around with my Cavalier?"

"It must be Tony Lewis," Suzanne said and pointed to a vehicle parked along the street. "He's the only guy I know who drives a red Jeep."

Tony? Her pulse did a strange little dance. She hadn't been able to get him off her mind since they met yesterday afternoon.

"It *is* Tony!" Cody unbuckled his seatbelt and began to bounce up and down in his seat. "Let's go, Mom! I wanna talk to Tony!"

"It's Tony!" Lily repeated and tried to imitate Cody's body movements, but instead she lost her balance and fell backwards into the soft leather.

Merry dug into her tote bag and pulled out a couple bills. She opened the car door then quickly reached over and shoved the money

34

into Suzanne's hand. "Thanks for taking me to pick up the kids from school. You know how much I appreciate it."

Suzanne's thick red hair and round, freckled face reminded Merry of a live Jessie doll. She moved faster than Buzz Lightyear, though, and demonstrated it by stuffing the cash back into Merry's bag. "Keep the money, sweetie. You need it to get your car fixed."

Cody and Lily exited on the passenger side and ran across the yard to see Tony.

"Are we still on for tomorrow night?" Suzanne's bright green eyes pierced hers. "I'll bring a couple steaks to throw on the grill."

"Yum...you bet we are. I'll make a salad and bake some potatoes."

Suzanne waved to Tony while she talked. "And we're going to search through Aidan's storage boxes after dinner, right?"

Merry paused, questioning for the umpteenth time the wisdom of continuing this exercise in futility. "I don't see what good it will do. I've already been through Aidan's things several times and found nothing even remotely resembling a clue to where he might have hidden the money. I keep hoping I've missed something—a detail of some sort, but I haven't come across anything useful."

"Don't worry, if he unwittingly left any evidence leading to the whereabouts of that money, we'll find it. You *have* to get it back. Aidan has it stashed somewhere and when he gets out of prison, he's going to take it and run." Suzanne flashed a wide, toothy grin. "With any luck, we'll get to it first!" She waved goodbye. "I'm late. See you at work tomorrow!"

Merry barely shut the door before Suzanne drove off to her hair appointment. As she watched her childhood friend disappear over the Nicollet Street Bridge, she wondered if they were simply wasting their time. She'd combed through Aidan's personal property when he first went to prison, desperate to find a key, a scrap of paper...anything that might help guide her to where he'd hidden the money, but the search turned up nothing. A daunting, if not impossible task—she understood that, but she also knew that if anyone could find a lead in that pile of junk-filled boxes stacked in her basement, Suzanne could. Perhaps Suzanne would see something she'd glossed over, a simple clue hiding in plain sight.

She turned toward the house to locate the kids and saw them clustered around their new friend and pizza supplier, Tony Lewis. Both were excitedly chattering at once.

She found Tony hunched over the engine of her two-door coupe, wrench in hand. "Thank you for the pizza last night. The kids really enjoyed it." She glanced down at the engine. "What are you doing to my car?"

He wore faded jeans and a white T-shirt under his dark hoodie. At the sound of her voice, he straightened, deep concentration creasing his brow. The chilly breeze ruffled his thick, dark locks. "Do you have your car keys handy?"

She went still for a moment, taking in the lean, sharp angle of his jaw and the intense blue of his eyes. As his gaze melded with hers, her heart fluttered. "I...um...a-always carry my keys."

His eyes twinkled, tiny crinkles forming at the corners. "Good, let's see if it'll start."

Really? Oh, my gosh...

Merry slid into the driver's seat and gingerly inserted her key into the ignition switch. She pushed in the clutch and turned the key. The engine started immediately; no e-r-r-r-r, no click-click-click, just a nice, sweet purr.

She sat back and stared through the windshield at Tony's wide grin, amazed at what he'd accomplished. She smiled back, relieved to have her car running again. She desperately needed to shop for groceries. More importantly, though, now she didn't have to bother Suzanne for a ride home from work on Saturday night.

Cody opened the passenger door and climbed into the back seat. "Let's go get some pizza, Mom!"

Lily took her usual place in her car seat on the passenger side. "I wanna go to Grandma's house."

Tony opened the door on her side and leaned in to check the gauges on the dashboard. "Let it run for a little while."

She shifted the car into neutral. "I don't know what you did to get it running again, but thank you so much!"

Their faces were so close they could almost kiss. In fact, she wanted to kiss him out of sheer happiness. She gazed at his wide, sensual lips and, for a moment, entertained the urge to move closer...

As if sensing her thoughts, his gaze intensified, but the temptation vanished when Cody's foot kicked the back of her seat, reminding her that the kids were in the car. She cleared her throat and pulled back, putting a respectable distance between her and Tony.

"It didn't take much, just a new battery and better-quality cables," Tony said as he shoved his wrench into a back pocket of his jeans. "Oh, and I figured it probably needed new plugs and plug wires, so I changed them, too."

Realizing he'd spent his own money on the parts brought her back to reality. "How much did everything cost? I intend to pay you for this."

He straightened. "I got a good deal on the battery. Plugs and cables don't cost much. I'd say roughly two hundred for everything."

Two hundred dollars? She almost swallowed her tongue. "I'll pay you back every penny, but it's going to take a little while. I didn't expect—I have to make my house payment first."

"There's no hurry." Tony shrugged. "I'm not worried about it."

The ease with which he brushed it off made her blush. "You have no idea what this means to me. Are you always this nice?"

He hesitated, as though weighing his response. "Only to the people I like," he replied softly.

A thump against her seat made Merry glance into the rear view mirror. Cody sat watching them, his face scrunched up, his brows knit together, as though sensing a current flowing between them that he didn't understand.

"Cody," Tony burst out and gestured toward the garage, "go and open the overhead door so your mom can park her car in there."

Cody met Tony at the front of the car and pointed toward the garage. "The big door? But...it's broken."

"Not any more. Try it."

Cody ran to the garage and disappeared through the service door. In a couple moments, the overhead began to glide upward.

Lily pointed toward the garage. "Lookit, Momma!"

Tony motioned for Merry to pull the car into the building. She shifted into first gear and slowly drove into her garage. It only took Tony one day to fix something she'd been going without for months. She suddenly wished Gerald Grange had decided to sell the contract a long time ago.

He held open the car door for her and extended his hand to help her out. "I hope you don't mind my tinkering with your property when you're not around. I just want you to be safe coming home from work at night."

Merry took Tony's hand and slid out of the car. The gentle strength of his fingers clasped around hers sent tingles across her palm, spreading warmth up her arm. "How did you know what to do to fix it?" Feeling self-conscious, she turned back and unlatched the safety belt on Lily's car seat. "My dad used to fix everything for me, but he's disabled now and can't do much."

"Many of my rental properties are older duplexes." Tony shut the car door after they got out of the vehicle and walked them to the service entrance. "I own about twenty-five now and it's a constant battle to keep the places in good repair. My Jeep has become my second garage, holding all the tools I need. I pay a handyman to do most of the specialized work, but occasionally a job calls for two people so I lend him a hand." He reached out and pressed the activation switch, paying close attention to the rollers as the overhead door slowly slid down the steel track. "I've learned a lot about general maintenance from him."

"Wow," Cody exclaimed, "you must be rich!"

Tony laughed. "No, I owe money on every property."

Merry grabbed Lily by the hand. "How did you get so many?"

He turned to her. "I'm a licensed realtor. Whenever I come across a decent rental property for the right price, I pick it up. I started working in the real estate market to put myself through college, but it eventually evolved into a full-time business."

They walked toward the back steps of the house. "I met your neighbor," Tony said, changing the subject.

"You mean, Katie Flynn?"

"Yeah," Tony replied with a chuckle. "She saw me walk into your garage and came right over, demanding to know what I was doing here. I introduced myself and showed her the parts I came to replace. She ended up lending me a ladder."

"Her father, Charlie, owns the house, but he's in the hospital right now." Merry's heart squeezed with a pang of guilt at not making time to visit Grandpa Charlie. "He had a heart attack and he doesn't know how long he's going to be laid up so he wants her to take over his horse-drawn carriage business."

"He has a horse?" Tony stared at the Flynn house. "Where does he keep it?"

They reached the back door. Merry pulled her keys out of her coat pocket. "All I know is that it's somewhere close by. His carriage is stored in the garage." She splayed the key ring on her palm, searching for the house key. "The problem is that Katie is a professor at a college in Ohio. She needs to get back there soon, so she doesn't want to start something she can't finish." Merry looked up. "Still, I think it would be fun to get a carriage ride out of her before she went back to Columbus."

Lily tugged on the edge of Tony's jacket. "Tony, Tony, are you going to eat supper at our house?"

Tony patted her blonde head. "No, cutie, I have to get going." He turned to Merry. "I have an appointment to show a vacant unit to a couple in about an hour."

Merry tucked Lily's neck scarf inside her jacket. "We don't have anything to make for supper, honey! I have to get my grocery list and coupons from the kitchen so we can go shopping. Gosh, I shouldn't have parked the car in the garage after all."

She looked up, realizing she needed to get her debt settled before Tony left. "Seriously, Tony, I appreciate all you've done for me today, but we need to agree on how I'm going to pay you back. I can give you money on a weekly basis, if that works for you."

He didn't answer at first. Instead, he pulled the wrench out of his pocket and walked over to his toolbox, dropping it in.

Please don't ask me to pay you back all of the money now...

"I've got a better idea," he said thoughtfully and flipped the top of the toolbox closed, latching it. "I need someone to board my dog for a couple weeks." He looked Merry in the eyes, as though challenging her to object. "I'll supply the food."

"Wow!" Cody hopped around like a frog, beside himself with excitement. "Can we, Mom? Can we, pleaaaaase?"

Lily's eyes widened like saucers. "You have a *dog*? What kind of a dog is it?"

Tony rubbed the back of his neck, looking perplexed. "Um...not sure, but it's good with kids."

Merry paused with her hand on the screen door. "Tony, I don't know if that's such a good idea. This place isn't set up for a dog. I don't have a fenced-in yard for it to run. What if I let it out to go potty and it runs away? Besides, we're gone all day and the dog would have to stay in the house all alone."

The kids crowded around her, vying for her attention as they pestered her to take the dog.

"My house is empty during the day, too. The way I see it, the dog would be better off spending its evenings and weekends playing with a couple rambunctious kids than watching sports on television with a single guy." Tony picked up his toolbox. "Just take the dog for a month and help me out. Please, Merry? I'll consider it an even exchange."

He'd made her an offer she couldn't refuse and they both knew it.

She sighed. "Okay, I'll give it a try, but I'm not promising anything. If the dog chews the furniture or pees on the floor, you're getting it back," she said, though she knew she should have demanded to see the dog first. Something didn't seem quite right when he acted as though he didn't know the dog's breed. Why wouldn't he offer that information? She only hoped it didn't turn out to be a slobbering, pile-pooping monster...

****

Tony stood in the doorway of Sam's Bar and scanned the boisterous crowd of happy-hour revelers, looking for the scrooge in the room—Neal Carter. This meeting wouldn't resemble anything close to a social call, but he had to go through with it because he needed to set the record straight about Merry Connor and move on. Convincing Neal to do the same would be like trying to drain Lake Superior with a garden hose, but at this point, he didn't care. He simply wanted to end this ridiculous ruse and leave.

He spied Neal sitting in a corner booth, wearing jeans and a green and white Minnesota Wild hockey jersey, relishing a plate of beef nachos. He squared his shoulders and crossed the room, wishing he'd delivered the news over the phone as he'd originally planned to do instead of agreeing to meet for a drink. Silently, he slid into the booth, keeping his jacket on, his white-knuckled hands clenching together at his sides.

"How'd it go?" Neal didn't bother to look up, preferring to focus on shoving a large chip covered with melted cheddar cheese and jalapeños into his mouth.

"She's innocent."

Neal choked on his food and broke into a fit of coughing, his face turning crimson. He grabbed his water glass and chugged several deep gulps. Then he drew in a deep breath. "What did you say?"

"Merry Connor is innocent," Tony said with finality. "She had nothing to do with her ex-husband's crime."

Neal looked up, piercing him with a stone-faced glare. "This time last week you didn't even know her, but now you're an expert on her character? You haven't spent enough time with her to determine what she is capable of doing."

Tony ignored Neal's comments and turned his attention to the slender blonde server in jeans and a white blouse approaching their table. She set a cardboard coaster in front of him and smiled. "What would you like to drink?"

At another time, perhaps, he would have found her fuzzy red and white Santa hat and necklace of blinking Christmas lights amusing, but today he merely shook his head. "Nothing, thanks. I'm not going to be here long."

As soon as she left them alone, he focused on Neal again, eager to speak his piece and get out of there. "Given my experience in dealing with people, I'd say I'm an excellent judge of character." He paused in disgust, watching Neal shove another gooey chip into his mouth. "I've seen her place; it's garage sale central. She drives an old beater, still uses a flip phone and her second-hand television set is a picture tube model hooked up to rabbit ears. Merry Connor is not sitting on top of a million dollars. She's broke."

"It's a smokescreen," Neal argued sarcastically. "She's biding her time, playing the victim until the old man gets out of prison. Then they'll turn into the Beverly Hillbillies." He snorted. "California—here we come!"

"That's not true. Merry is a hard-working woman who's struggling to make ends meet. She's endured more hardship than anyone affected by this crime."

"Don't try to protect her."

"I'm telling you what I saw! Look, Neal, we agreed—"

"We *agreed* you would get the truth out of her," Neal countered with authority, as though reprimanding one of his employees. "Now get back over there and *do your job*."

No one could aggravate him like his brother-in-law. For a moment, Tony went rigid as he envisioned smashing that plate of nachos into Neal's face.

Let it go. He's not worth it...

Tony sat back and drew in a deep breath, refusing to allow Neal's arrogance get to him. "I've done what we agreed to and given you my assessment of the situation. My decision stands. As far as I'm concerned, it's over."

"You've got it bad for her, don't you?" Neal scowled. "Did you sleep with her? Is that how she got to you?"

A couple descriptive and highly offensive four-letter words perched on the edge of Tony's tongue, but he stopped himself before letting them fly. He would not stoop to Neal's level, no matter how much the man baited him. "Actually, her kids got to me," he said, purposely sidestepping the subject of his friendship with Merry. "They've suffered more than anyone. They lost their father, their home and a stable family life. Instead of judging Merry, it's time someone in our family reached out to her and showed her kids some kindness. If it were my son in that position, I'd want the same for him."

"Well, I'll be—are you saying you've finally gotten off that high horse of self-pity you've been straddling for the last three years? You've decided to think about someone else besides your pathetic self for a change?" Neal followed up with a sharp, derisive laugh. "I won't believe that until I see it with my own eyes." He shoved away the congealing, half-eaten plate of nachos and grabbed his beer. "In any case, I guess it's time to hire another P. I. to finish the job since you're not man enough to do it."

Tony slid out of the booth and stood, towering over Neal. "Say whatever you want about me; I could care less, but leave Merry Connor alone. She has a right to her privacy."

Neal raised his beer in a mock salute. "Look who's talking! Do you really think she'll be in a forgiving mood when she finds out *you've* violated her privacy?"

"I fully intend to disclose my connection to you and Faith,"

Tony said, "but as far as I'm concerned, I haven't done anything wrong. I bought the contract-for-deed and met with the contract holder. There is absolutely nothing illegal or inappropriate about either action."

Neal glared at him. "I'll bet she'd find it extremely inappropriate if she learned your only motive for doing those things was to get justice for your sister."

"I'm warning you." Tony stabbed a finger in Neal's direction, coming close to his brother-in-law's face. "Stay away from Merry or else. That goes for the watchdog you're going to hire, too. I don't want him anywhere near her property or her kids. Cross that line and you'll both answer to *me*." He turned and walked away, resolute to make good on his threat if Neal didn't back off.

As he left the bar, the song "Have Yourself a Merry Little Christmas" followed him onto the empty, snow-dusted patio. He hadn't experienced a "merry little Christmas" since his wife and son died, but that didn't mean he couldn't bring joy to someone else's holiday. Joy— the kind that came with four legs, a wet nose and a wagging tail.

The thought of Merry and the kids lifted his mood considerably. He'd given her the option to "board his dog" in lieu of cash for the car parts as an excuse to see her again. He wanted to see her again, very much so, but knew he needed to reveal his connection to Neal and Faith to her as soon as possible. That said, he couldn't just walk up to Merry and blurt it out. No, he'd have to find a way to talk to her without the kids around so he could break it to her gently. He needed to tell her the truth, but at the same time, he wanted to convince her that the situation between Aidan and the Carters would never affect their friendship.

He turned up the collar of his jacket and bounded down the stairs, stepping onto the cobblestone sidewalk of St. Anthony Main. Light, feathery flakes floated through the air, clinging to his coat and hair as he passed offices and shops draped with pine garland and red velvet bows. He stopped in front of Pracna on Main, a historic restaurant that had been in operation since 1890, to browse the menu posted in a glass case.

This would be a nice place to take Merry for dinner.

For the first time since Cherie's death, Tony had allowed himself to become attracted to another woman. Ever since they met, Merry Connor had been on his mind and the more he thought about her, the more the sadness of losing Cherie slowly lifted. He couldn't stop thinking about Merry's radiant smile, the sparkle in her eyes when she laughed and the soft lilt in her voice whenever she spoke to him. He wanted to have dinner with her on Saturday night, just the two of them, but would she even want to be friends once she learned his sister and brother-in-law were responsible for sending her husband to jail?

He shoved his hands into his jacket pockets and walked on. Leveling with Merry was a risk he was willing to take.

Chapter 4

December 6th

"Look, Momma!"

Merry walked into the living room wiping her soapy hands on a kitchen towel. She and Suzanne had washed the dinner dishes and cleaned the kitchen while Cody and Lily decorated the tree. As soon as they checked on the kids, however, they planned to go down to the basement to search through the storage boxes containing the remnants of Aidan's personal property. Merry had called a Veteran's charity to pick up most of his possessions when the bank repossessed their home, holding back only his best clothes and personal papers. She had always intended to give the boxes to his mother, but until now had put it off. On one hand, she wanted to get his things out of her house, but on the other hand, the thought of doing *anything* for that man repelled her.

Suzanne had insisted on investigating the contents of the boxes, stubbornly believing he'd left something behind that would lead them to the stolen money. Merry had already combed through them twice and hadn't found a single clue, but she agreed that perhaps someone with a different perspective on the situation would see a possibility in something she'd overlooked.

Lily stood next to the second-hand artificial spruce Merry had picked up at a thrift store and pointed toward her first attempt at trimming a Christmas tree. She'd covered the bottom half with all the ornaments and plastic icicles. Other than a string of multi-colored mini-lights Cody had haphazardly wound around the branches, the top half stood bare.

"That's...um...pretty..." Merry said as she stared at the tree.

Suzanne stood behind her. "Good job, princess!" She placed her hands on her hips and studied Lily's masterpiece. "Did you do this all by yourself?"

Lily's head bobbed vigorously as she beamed with satisfaction. She'd clustered all of the gold balls in one area, the red balls in another. At her eye level, she'd hung the blue ones in a straight line. The tree looked peculiar, but Lily hadn't looked this happy in a long time and the sight of her daughter's proud smile warmed Merry's heart.

Cody slid off the sofa where he'd spent the last half-hour stretched out on a pillow, watching his favorite television show. "It looks dumb."

Lily stamped her foot. "No, it don't!"

He walked over to the tree and grabbed an ornament, pulling it off.

"No!" Lily lunged at him, trying to retrieve the shiny red ball. "Don't touch it!"

He pushed her hand away and reached for another one, but Merry interceded, pulling the two apart.

"Let it be, Cody." Merry took the ball from her son as Suzanne hugged Lily. She hung the ball where Lily had originally placed it and turned back to Cody. "I'll get some more ornaments this week and you can decorate the top half, all right? But for now, we'll enjoy it the way she's arranged it."

"Okay, but it looks weird..." Cody stomped back to the sofa and flopped across it, staring at the television. "If my friends see it, they'll laugh at me."

"I'll get more. I promise."

He shrugged, but refused to answer.

His attitude and uncooperative behavior saddened her. Losing his father had been hard on him. She understood that, but she didn't know how to fill the gap Aidan's absence had created. She crossed the room and sat down next to him. "What's the matter, Cody? Are you lonesome for Daddy?"

He looked down at his lap and nodded. The sight of his unhappiness, especially at Christmastime, wrenched her heart. She slid her arms around him and held him close. "I'm sorry, honey. Someday you'll see him again, but for now, we still have each other. We'll do the best we can with what we have. Okay?"

Cody nodded again and sighed, but pulled away. "I'm hungry."

This kid is a bottomless pit. He had supper less than an hour ago...

"Would you like some chicken nuggets? There are some left in the freezer." She had grilled the steaks Suzanne brought, but made Cody and Lily their favorite meal—burgers and fries.

His face lit up at the offer of another one of his favorite foods. "Yeah—can I have a lot of ketchup, too?"

Relieved to see his jubilance return, she mentally sighed with relief. The way to this little man's heart always led through his stomach. "Okay, I'll be right back." She went into the kitchen and heated the food in the microwave. "Here you go," she said, coming

49

back into the living room with the chicken, a small dish of ketchup and a glass of milk. She didn't allow the kids to eat in the living room, but made an exception today. "Suzanne and I are going to be busy in the basement for a while and I'm counting on you to get along with your sister while we're downstairs. If I hear any fighting, you two are going straight to your rooms. Do you understand?"

"Yeah," he said and stuffed a nugget in his mouth.

Merry went into the dining room and found Suzanne helping Lily wrap the gifts she'd made in school. Suzanne pushed her chair away from the table and stood as Merry entered. "Cody is watching television and he's been warned to behave, so I'm ready to go downstairs and get started," Merry said.

"Everything is set here, too." Suzanne patted Lily on the head and placed her other hand on a small roll of blue foil paper, steadying it so the child could chop off a piece with her rounded-edge scissors. "Lily has important work to do here, don't you sweetie?"

Lily cut a crooked piece, grinning as she worked with the diligence of a busy bee.

Merry went into the kitchen, propped open the basement door and headed down the narrow wooden stairs, switching on the light as she went. Suzanne followed close behind. Twelve cardboard storage boxes of Aidan's personal effects were stacked in a corner across the room.

Suzanne stood with her hands on her hips, surveying the lot. "What's in them?"

Merry turned one on the top row toward her to read the description of the contents written with a black felt-tip pen. "The boxes on top contain Aidan's best clothes and shoes. The heavy ones on the floor are full of his personal papers. I gave everything else to the Veterans."

50

Suzanne grabbed a box of clothing off the top of the stack. "Aidan is lucky you didn't give it all away. You're nicer than I would have been if I'd found myself in your situation."

Merry set the next box on a card table. She pulled the lid off and held up a blue tweed sport jacket. "I plan to cart the whole stack over to his mother's house next spring and pile them in her garage. The building is full of Aidan's tools and small engines, anyway."

Suzanne set her box next to Merry's on the table. Together, she and Merry combed through every piece of clothing, searching the pockets and checking the linings for a scrap of paper, a receipt, a key or a business card that might give them insight where to look next.

"Gosh, it's been a long time since I've been in this basement. This house holds a lot of memories for me," Suzanne said as she pulled out a black hoodie and turned out the pockets. "Remember when I used to come here in the summer to stay with Aunt Eleanor? I spent a lot of time with her in the kitchen learning to bake and can vegetables from her garden." Suzanne sighed wistfully. "My heart will always hold a special place for this old house. I love it so much."

"I love this house, too, and I'll never sell it." Merry dumped another box of clothes onto the table and began searching through each piece, folding them as she put them back into the container. "It has so much character. I'm glad the State of Minnesota designated this island as historic because it means the area will stay preserved forever."

"I knew you wouldn't want to leave this place once you got settled into the neighborhood and that's why I argued with Gerald to sell this property to you on terms you could afford. He got sick of fighting with me and gave me what I wanted." Suzanne pulled a small Allen wrench and a couple bolts from the pocket of a thin beige jacket. She set them on the table and refolded the garment. "I couldn't bear the thought of giving up this place, but I didn't have the money to buy him out, so I figured if you bought it, that was the next best thing I could do to keep it in my life."

Merry tucked the last article of clothing back in her box and closed the lid. "I'll admit I was disappointed when you guys sold the contract to Tony Lewis. When Tony called and wanted to meet with me to review the terms, I didn't like the idea at all. I thought he might pressure me to sell out, but he didn't even mention it."

"How's that going? I mean, he repaired your car so I assume you two have become good friends." Suzanne gave her a fixed stare. "He *is* single and unattached, isn't he? The last thing you need right now is to get mixed up with a married man."

Merry grabbed another box and dumped the contents on the table. "He mentioned he has a son, but I know he's not married." She held up a cream-colored linen shirt, covered with dark green palm leaves. "When he told me I could board his dog instead of paying him the two hundred he spent on car parts, he made a point of saying the animal would be better off staying in a house with kids than living with a single guy." She folded the shirt and set it on top of a stack on the table. "Whether or not he's unattached is another story."

Suzanne laughed. "Well, I have to admit, taking care of his pooch is a better idea than paying the money. What kind of dog is it? I hope it's good with kids."

Merry stopped, accidentally dropping a pair of cargo shorts back into the box. "Well, that's a mystery." She rested her wrists on the edge of the carton. "He gave a vague description when I pressed him about it." She frowned, recalling the conversation. "He said it was good with kids."

"That's all?"

"Yeah."

"I hope he's not using you to rid himself of a problem pet that whizzes on the nearest rug or barks all day." Suzanne closed the lid on her box and set it on the floor. "So, what did you tell him? Did you accept his offer?"

"Of course I did." Merry picked up the cargo shorts and jammed her hands into the pockets, hoping to find something useful, but instead found an old grocery receipt. "What choice do I have? I sure as heck don't have the money to pay him." She crumbled up the receipt and tossed it in the box. "He said he'd buy the dog's food."

"That means he'll be dropping by occasionally to see his pet and bring more chow." Suzanne's freckled face produced a know-it-all smirk. "It sounds to me like he purposely came up with that plan for an excuse to see you on a regular basis."

"He's probably just helping me out because he feels sorry for me and he wants to make sure I have transportation to work so I make my house payment on time," Merry said wryly, but remembered him saying he only did nice things for people he liked. Then...he must *like* her, but how much? She shrugged and dug deeper into the box. "He's very attractive. What woman wouldn't like a tall, dark and handsome man who can fix things and who likes dogs and kids? The problem is...I'm not looking for a man. I have enough issues right now just trying to get my life in order. I certainly don't have time to start dating anyone. Besides, it'll be a long time before I trust anyone again."

Suzanne reached into her box and held up a small key. "Hey, what's this?"

Merry glanced at it then resumed her work. "That's just a key to Aidan's tool chest. I came across it the last time I searched that box, too. It's nothing to get excited about."

"Shouldn't you keep it in a safe place for him?"

"No, all Aidan keeps in that old relic is his dad's screwdrivers and wrenches. I don't know if he even bothers to lock it. Last time I checked, it was empty."

Suzanne curiously glanced around the room. "Where is it?"

"It's at his mother's house in her garage with the rest of his junk."

"Oh." Suzanne dropped the key back in the box and continued with her search.

Merry and Suzanne spent the next twenty minutes rummaging through Aidan's clothes then started on the boxes filled with paperwork. They found receipts, old warranties, assembly instructions, product guarantees, operating manuals and paid repair bills, but no clues. Other boxes contained income tax filings, property tax filings, old abstracts, real estate paperwork and auto repair books.

Suzanne pulled out a brown accordion folder stuffed with receipts and burial information in the last box marked "Wills and Funeral Arrangements." She set the square-bottomed folder on the card table and thumbed through the papers. "Aidan was so organized." She pulled out a small collection of funeral memorials. "Who are all these people?"

Merry began sorting and restacking the boxes strewn across the floor, lining the bottom row with the heaviest ones. "They're for Aidan's father and a couple spinster aunts. Aidan held power of attorney to handle his aunts' affairs when they were alive. As administrator of their wills, he arranged the funerals and disbursed their possessions once they passed away."

Suzanne glanced up from her paperwork with a cynical look.

Merry chuckled. "I know what you're thinking and no, he didn't steal money from them. His aunts lived on small pensions that barely sustained them. His father's money is invested in a joint account with his mother's and Aidan can't touch it."

Suzanne stuffed the memorials back into the accordion folder and went to place it back in the box when Merry stopped her.

"I should probably give that folder to Aidan's mother. Why don't you leave it on the table and the next time I take the kids over to see Rosella, I'll bring it with me."

Suzanne slumped into a folding chair as Merry replaced the top on the box and set it on the growing stack in the corner. "Well, you were right. We didn't find a single clue." She smacked her hand on the table. "There has to be something we missed! Are you sure we searched every box?" At Merry's nod, she glanced around, resting her gaze on the Allen wrench. "Wait a minute." She looked up. "You said Aidan has an entire garage of stuff."

Merry halted, holding a box. "I said he had a garage full of junk."

Suzanne's eyes lit up. "Have you searched through it?"

"I've poked around inside the building, yes, but there isn't anywhere in that garage he could store a million dollars."

Suzanne jumped out of her chair. "It's worth taking another look at. Come on."

Merry set the box down and tucked a loose strand of hair behind her ear. "Are you saying you want to go over there tonight?"

"Yeah," Suzanne replied in a singsong tone, "why not?" She glanced at her phone. "It's only seven-thirty. Is that too late for your ex-mother-in law?"

"Actually, it's not." Merry shrugged. "Rosella's a night owl." She gestured toward the remainder of Aidan's boxes strewn about the floor. "We could bring some of these to store in the garage as an excuse to come over. Rosella has been asking me to bring the kids around anyway. She wants to give them their Christmas gifts." Merry rolled her eyes, though not in a condescending way. She had always gotten along well with Aidan's widowed mother. "She has all of her holiday shopping done by August."

Suzanne grabbed the closest box. "I could get probably six of these in the back of my SUV. I'll start hauling them out while you set up the visit."

Merry grabbed a box and followed Suzanne upstairs, grateful someone had pushed her into getting rid of Aidan's things by offering a helping hand. In the kitchen, she set the box on the table and went into the living room to talk to the kids. "Who wants to go to Grandma Connor's house to get their Christmas presents?"

Cody jumped off the sofa, cheering. "I do!" Lily ran to her and followed suit.

Merry went back to the dining room and dug her phone from her purse to call Rosella. "Cody, help Lily get her coat on. We're riding with Suzanne," she said while she waited for her call to go through. "Hello, Rosella! This is Merry..."

By the time Suzanne returned, Merry had hung up. "Rosella said tonight isn't a good time to drop by. She's hosting a Christmas party for her quilting club." Merry set the phone on the kitchen counter. "Tomorrow she's going out of town for a few days to visit a cousin in Florida, but she wants to have us over for dinner next Thursday so she can give the kids their gifts."

Suzanne's buoyant mood deflated. "Well, then I guess I'll unload the car."

The search would have to wait for another time.

Chapter 5

December 8th

On Thursday evening, Tony pulled his Jeep into the parking lot of a beige, single-story building and curiously stared through the windshield at the "Homeward Bound" sign above the door. He'd never visited an animal shelter before, but had chosen this place on the recommendation of a client who'd assured him all the dogs waiting for adoption were in good health. At first, it had seemed like a crazy idea to get a dog, but the more he thought about it, the more it made sense. He knew how much Merry's kids wanted one and asking Merry to board it would provide an easy way for her to reimburse him the two hundred he'd spent to fix her car. He didn't want the money back, but Merry's independent spirit would never allow her to accept his generosity as a gift, so he'd come up with an alternative plan to benefit everyone. Once she'd paid him back in boarding fees, he planned to give the dog to the kids as a Christmas present.

Satisfied with his decision, he locked his vehicle and went into the shelter, determined to find the perfect companion for Cody and Lily.

Pungent odors of disinfectant assaulted his senses as he pulled open the door. The small, square lobby reminded him of a veterinary clinic with padded benches, posters of pets "in waiting" lining the walls and a large shelving unit containing an assortment of pet items for sale. As he approached the service counter, the loud, unsynchronized clamor of dogs barking echoed from a back room. A young, dark-haired woman wearing the Homeward Bound uniform of jeans and a forest green polo bearing the "HB" emblem sat behind a Formica counter, giving someone information over the phone about dropping off an animal at the shelter. He checked his own phone for messages while he waited.

"May I help you?" the girl asked with a smile as she hung up.

"I called this afternoon about viewing your dogs for adoption."

"Yes, I remember speaking with you." She picked up the handset again. "Your name, sir?"

"Tony," he said. "Tony Lewis."

"One moment, please." She punched in a couple numbers and spoke to someone. Almost immediately, a middle-aged woman came through a side door on his right.

"Good afternoon, Mr. Lewis and welcome to Homeward Bound. I'm Sharleen," she said in a friendly voice and shook his hand. "I'll be assisting you today in finding the right pet." She opened the door and stood aside. "Would you step this way please?"

He followed the brown-haired woman into a long, high-ceilinged warehouse. As they came through the door, cats of all sizes and colors watched him through the wire fronts of their cages.

"This is our kitty corner," Sharleen said, pointing to an L-shaped area housing the felines.

"You have a lot of animals here," Tony said, taking in the huge number of cages and kennels in the facility.

"Homeward Bound is a 'no-kill' shelter and we have an open admission policy which means we accept every animal that is surrendered to us. They receive examinations, vaccinations and medical treatments, if necessary. Then we microchip them and spay or neuter them if it's needed. I understand you're looking for a dog. Do you have a specific breed in mind?"

"I don't care what breed it is, actually, as long as it's good with kids."

She nodded. "How many children do you have?"

"Ah...two, girl and boy," he said, wanting to keep things simple, "ages six and nine."

She turned and gestured toward several long corridors of tall kennels constructed of chain link fencing. "The dogs are in this area. If you find an animal you're interested in and you'd like to spend some time with it, I'll be glad to assist you."

"Thank you," Tony replied, barely hearing his own words. As he focused on the array of kennels, a profound sadness began to overtake him. He understood that shelters were necessary to house orphaned animals who would otherwise be struggling for food and cover on the streets. However, the sight of so many desperate and homeless pets made him realize the seriousness of the problem and he made a mental note to thank his client for urging him to seek out this facility rather than going to a breeder. In a few minutes, he'd possess one happy pooch and the shelter would have one less mouth to feed, one less body taking up precious space.

He strolled along the nearest corridor, searching for something suitable for Cody and Lily. Almost immediately, the thunderous roar ricocheting off the cinderblock walls and the sheer number of dogs barking, whining and jumping against their cages overwhelmed him. He passed pit bulls of every color, German shepherds, Labrador mixes and many others he found impossible to identify. Some kennels housed only one dog, others held several, all watching him pass by, their sorrowful cries piercing his ears as they stared up at him, begging for attention.

I wish I could take them all home, he thought as he locked eyes with a black Lab and saw the animal's heart-wrenching desperation, *but I can only rescue one.*

At the end of the corridor, Tony came upon a medium-sized dog, white with a large patch of black fur on its back. It had a brown face with a black forehead and black ears. Though it had a bed, the canine lay curled up on the floor with its back to the gate, its chin resting between its white paws.

"What's the matter, little guy? Is all this noise getting to you, too?" He knelt to get a better look, but the dog ignored him. The animal's listlessness and complete withdrawal from its surroundings gave Tony the impression it had given up hope. The thought tugged at his heart. He signaled to Sharleen. "What's wrong with this one?" he asked as she approached. "Is he ill?"

"If you're asking about the Jack Russell terrier, he's in fine health, but he's homesick. He's been mourning the loss of his owner since the family dropped him off." She scanned the information card fastened to his cage. "Chauncey is three years old, neutered and obedience-trained."

The thought of someone simply discarding a pet made Tony angry. "Why would anyone abandon him?"

She knelt and slipped her hand into the kennel. As she stroked the dog's back, he gazed up at them, with large, sad eyes. "Chauncey's story is all too common, I'm afraid." She looked up at Tony. "His owner died and no one in the elderly man's family wanted to take him so they surrendered him to us. He's a sweet little dog and I give him as much attention as I can, but he's still having a difficult time adjusting."

Tony couldn't pull his gaze away from the terrier. He knew the emptiness and utter loneliness of losing a loved one and his empathy drew him even closer to the dog. "Are you saying, then, that I can't have this one?"

"Oh, not at all." Sharleen stood. "The final choice is yours. I simply wanted to let you know that Chauncey belonged to an older person who lived alone so he may not be used to children."

Disappointed, Tony gave the little guy one last look and moved on.

But he couldn't find another dog that seemed right for the kids. Many were large breeds or breeds with bad reputations and he knew Merry would balk if he brought one of those dogs to her house. She didn't favor the idea of caring for a canine when he suggested it, so he knew he needed to choose wisely.

If I were searching for a pet for my own son, what kind of dog would I select?

The Jack Russell terrier's soft brown eyes flashed into his mind...

After a half-hour of fruitless pacing, he decided to call it quits. Perhaps he could try another shelter in the metropolitan area, such as the Humane Society in Golden Valley. Unfortunately, he didn't have enough time to get there before the facility closed. Disillusioned, he left the shelter and drove home.

Later that night at home, Tony sat in front of his computer, searching through the photos of dogs on the Humane Society's website, but nothing he saw even remotely appealed to him. There were plenty of candidates to choose from; some were quite intriguing, but he couldn't get the image of the Jack Russell terrier out of his mind.

"Might as well admit it, I want that dog for Cody," he said aloud as he brought up the Homeward Bound website. "Chauncey may be suffering from loneliness now, but he won't be once he gets to

Merry's house." Tony searched through the shelter's photos, but the terrier wasn't among them. Had they found a home for Chauncey after he left? Tired and frustrated, he leaned back in his chair and rubbed the back of his neck, regretting his decision to walk away from the dog.

The next morning, Tony drove to the shelter early and waited in the parking lot for the facility to open. As soon as his watch read eight o'clock, he jumped out of the Jeep and marched inside the building. His apprehension mounted as he approached the young assistant he'd first spoken to yesterday afternoon. "I'm back to pick up the black and white terrier called Chauncey. Is he still here?"

"One moment, please," she said and picked up the phone. After a brief conversation, she hung up and informed him someone would be right with him, but ten minutes passed and the person hadn't appeared to show him into the back room. He'd begun to fear the worst when the side door opened and a teenage boy with short dark hair stepped through wearing the Homeward Bound uniform.

"Hi, I'm Jace." He extended his hand. "I apologize for the wait. We're short-handed today. Are you here to pick up a specific dog?"

Tony nodded and followed him toward the kennels.

"Which one did you decide upon?" Jace hollered over the noise.

"Back there," Tony replied and pointed toward the far end of the first corridor. "I want the terrier in the last pen."

But when they reached the narrow kennel, they found it abandoned. Tony's hopeful mood plummeted as confusion set in. What happened to Chauncey? Would he have to start the search for a dog all over again?

I should have taken him when I had the chance!

The teen stared at the empty space and thought for a moment. "I think the one we had in here has been moved." He turned and headed toward the next aisle with Tony on his heels.

To Tony's surprise, they found Chauncey in an area housing other small dogs. Filled with relief, he gazed upon the Connor kids' new dog and couldn't help smiling. He turned to Jace. "Would you open his kennel so I can get closer to him? I'd like to get to know him a little before I take him home."

"Sure, no problem." The teen unlocked the door and stood aside for Tony to enter. Instead of invading the dog's space, however, Tony simply knelt and offered Chauncey the back of his hand for inspection. The terrier timidly sniffed his long fingers then stared up at him.

"Hey there," Tony crooned softly and began to scratch the dog's soft ear. "You're a good boy, aren't you, buddy? I don't think you're a head case. I think you're just lonely." The dog wagged his white tail, enjoying the interaction.

Tony looked up at Jace. "Is he always as gentle as this? How does he behave with the people on staff?"

Jace reached down and petted the dog's back. "I haven't spent much time with this one, but he's never been a problem for me."

Tony scratched Chauncey under his chin. "How'd you like to bust out of here, huh? I think I can arrange it." He slowly rose to his feet and stepped away from the kennel. "What this dog needs is a family and I have a family that needs a dog, so I'm going to give him a chance. What's the process?"

"It's pretty simple," Jace said as he closed the kennel and locked it. "You fill out an application and then one of our adoption counselors will meet with you."

He led Tony to a small office to start the process. Once Tony finished with the application, an adoption counselor reviewed the key points of the contract with him and explained his thirty-day trial period. Since the deceased owner's family had surrendered him, Chauncey's packet contained his medical and personality information. Chauncey's profile revealed what Tony had suspected all along. The terrier had a good disposition and loved people. Tony paid for the dog along with a red collar-leash set and a mountain of dog food to give to Merry. He looked at car carriers, but decided Chauncey had spent enough time in a cage and bought a car harness instead.

The counselor met Tony in the lobby with Chauncey wearing his new equipment. "Congratulations on your new family addition, Mr. Lewis!" She handed him the red leather leash, a green cloth bag filled samples of dog treats and a folder containing his paperwork. "Please send us updates on how Chauncey is getting along in his new forever home. We look forward to hearing from you."

"Thank you. I'll email you some pictures of him with the kids as soon as he's had a chance to settle in." Tony waved goodbye and led Chauncey out of the building. Chauncey obediently trotted next to him, wagging his tail. Tony opened the Jeep's door and picked up the dog, depositing him in the passenger seat and clipping his car harness into the seatbelt receptacle. With mounting anticipation, he sprinted around the Jeep and hopped in.

"Okay, buddy, so here's the deal," he said to the dog as he shoved the key in the ignition and started the vehicle. "You're going to meet a couple of rambunctious kids this afternoon and I want you to be on your best behavior, okay?"

Chauncey's brown and black face merely stared up at him.

"Oh, and another thing—I'm changing your name. You need something with character; a name that fits your personality. I'm going to call you...well, I don't know yet, but I'll think of something by the time Merry and the kids get home this afternoon. In the meantime, let's go to the dog park and get some exercise. What do you say?"

The dog with no name leaned toward him and licked his hand.

"You're welcome." Tony shifted into reverse and backed out, looking forward to introducing the dog formerly known as Chauncey to a couple of very lucky kids.

****

Merry drove the car into her garage, relieved to be home from one of the toughest days she'd ever worked at the Inn. She planned to throw together a quick supper for the kids and after they went to bed, spend the rest of the evening off her tired, aching feet. She couldn't wait to sink into a warm tub filled with lavender bath salts and relax for a while. Then she'd snuggle under a thick comforter with a good book and a rich cup of cocoa. It sounded like heaven.

Her day had been busy to the point of craziness with multiple group luncheons, starting with a party of twenty raucous ladies from a local chapter of The Red Hat Club who requested separate checks and change for twenty-dollar bills. She had several smaller parties after that and a steady stream of customers until her shift ended at three o'clock. She'd barely managed to collect the money on all of her guest checks, complete her side work and turn in her checkout paperwork before rushing over to the school to pick up the kids on time.

As the garage's overhead door slowly descended, a movement in her rear view mirror caught her eye. She looked up and saw Tony's red Jeep roll into the driveway. Unfortunately, the kids saw him, too.

"Tony's here!" Cody unbuckled his seatbelt and lunged for the door handle.

"Cody Connor, stay in your seat until I shut off the car and tell you it's safe to get out!"

But her warning went unheeded. She gasped in horror as Cody grabbed his backpack and jumped out of the car. Faster than she could catch her breath, he dashed toward the overhead door and slipped under it. Luckily, the infrared motion detector worked properly and caused it to jolt to a stop. Frightened, she attempted to call out to him, but her words came out sounding like a hysterical squeak. As the door began to roll back up, she shut off the car and placed her hands over her thumping heart. "Oh, my gosh, that was close!" She drew in a deep breath, her fear turning to frustration. "When is that boy going to start *listening to me?*"

"Momma, help me," Lily cried, struggling with the safety belt on her car seat.

Merry unbuckled her daughter and lifted the child out of her car seat. "Come on, sweetie. Let's go see what's going on in the driveway. I can hear Cody whooping about something."

Keys in hand, she walked out of the garage to find Tony and Cody sitting on the back steps, a white dog with a large black patch on his back perched between them. The shorthaired dog had a cute brown face and black ears that perked up with curiosity upon her and Lily's approach. Merry noted the excitement in Cody's eyes as he showered his new friend with attention, alerting her that her intention to have a relaxing, low-key evening had just been derailed by four paws and a snout.

Well, at least it's not a St. Bernard.

Even so, she sighed with exhaustion at the thought of trying to care for another member of her household, especially one that needed a lot of attention. She approached the trio, shaking her finger. "Cody Connor, don't you *ever* do that again!"

"Hi," Tony said softly, rising to his feet, his snug-fitting jeans and dark brown bomber jacket hugging his tall, muscular frame. His eyes shone as their gazes met. "I hope you don't mind my dropping by without calling first."

She didn't mind at all, but she wished she'd had time to change out of her soiled uniform and into something decent before he showed up. Under her coat, au jus stains streaked her white oxford shirt and black slacks and she reeked of cooking grease. By now, her makeup had worn off, and her hair, bound in a granny knot on top of her head completed her fashion disaster. "No, I always look like this," she said, inadvertently thinking aloud.

"What?" His jaw dropped, as though disconcerted by her answer. "Is...is this a bad time?"

Merry winced at the stain of embarrassment rushing to his face. She hadn't meant to sound so cranky. "No, it's fine. I'm just worn out from a busy day, that's all." She selected the house key on her key ring and took Lily by the hand. "Let's go inside and warm up. Your dog is shivering. What's his name?" The blank stare in Tony's eyes made her pause on the step.

"Ah...his name...yeah," Tony said and looked around, his puzzled gaze lingering on the Flynn house next door. "It's—it's Charlie."

Cody laughed as he held the screen door open. "Did you hear that, Mom? I can't wait to show *our* Charlie to Grandpa Charlie!"

"He's not *our* Charlie," Merry snapped while shoving her key into the lock, "and if you don't start paying attention to what I say, he's not going to be staying with us, either!"

"Oh-oh," Tony said, his voice echoing over her head as he followed her and Lily into the kitchen. Cody picked up the rear with the terrier trailing at his heels. "Sounds like someone's in the doghouse and it isn't our Charlie."

Merry dropped her bag on the kitchen table and began to unbutton her coat. "Cody has gotten into the habit of doing what he wants to do rather than what he's supposed to do—like jumping out of the car before I shut it off and scooting under a moving garage door." She frowned at her son then slid out of her coat and helped Lily with hers. "I'm afraid one of these days he's going to pull a stunt that will result in serious consequences."

Cody hung his head. "I'm sorry, Mom."

Merry led everyone into the living room, her disillusionment growing with each step. Her hand shook as she opened the closet door and reached in for a hanger. Taking care of the dog had sounded doable at first, but common sense dictated that she shouldn't have agreed to it until she'd thought it through. In reality, she didn't have time to feed, care and keep track of a dog and couldn't trust Cody to handle the task without constant supervision. She couldn't think of a tactful way to back out, no excuse she could pass off as the truth, so she decided to simply level with Tony and settle the matter. It would upset him, but she couldn't prevent that.

Merry spun around, meeting him face to face, blinking back tears of fatigue and discouragement. "I'm sorry, Tony, but I'm afraid I can't take care of your dog after all."

"Are you serious?" Tony stared at her in disbelief, as though he hoped he'd misunderstood.

"Yes, unfortunately I am. I normally don't back out of my obligations at the last minute, but this time it's different." She wiped away the moisture from her eyes with the backs of her hands.

"Merry, what's wrong?"

"I'm concerned for Charlie's well-being. I just don't have the time to spend with him and I can't trust my kids to take care of him properly. Lily is too young and what happened in the garage a few minutes ago proves that Cody isn't mature enough to handle the responsibility, either."

Cody gasped and kneeled next to the dog, circling his arms around Charlie's neck. "*Mom!* Yes, I am! From now on, I'll do whatever you tell me to do. I promise!"

She turned to her son, unmoved by the shocked look in his eyes. "Promises aren't enough, Cody. You need to demonstrate to me that you can be trusted. So far, your behavior hasn't convinced me that you're grown up enough to handle caring for Charlie."

"But, Merry," Tony said slowly, "I was counting on you to take him until Christmas."

She paused, fighting back a surge of guilt over letting him down. "I'm truly sorry about that, but I shouldn't have agreed to it in the first place. Charlie needs better care than we can give him."

"Mom, don't say that! Please, give me a chance!" Now Cody's eyes brimmed with tears. "I'll take good care of Charlie. I will!" Still clutching the dog, he looked up at Tony. "You believe me, don't you?"

Lily reached up and tugged on the sleeve of Merry's shirt. "Please don't send Charlie home, Momma. Cody will be *so sad*. I'll be sad, too."

Tony reached out, placing his hands on the sides of Merry's shoulders, his thumbs gently massaging her muscles as his deep blue eyes searched hers.

"You're exhausted, aren't you?"

The steady, circular motion of his thumbs sent a flow of calm through her tensed, tired body. The muscles in her shoulders began to relax under the soothing power of his touch. Without thinking, she leaned toward him, yearning for more. She exhaled a deep sigh and mustered what little energy she had left to answer him with a short nod. Exhausted didn't begin to cover the wear and tear on her body at that moment.

"You need to get off your feet," he said and took her by the elbow, guiding her to the sofa. Placing his hands on her shoulders again, he slowly pressed her down on the cushions.

She rested her head against the back of her green plaid sofa and closed her eyes. "It was a madhouse at work today. I'm so tired I can hardly move."

Tony eased next to her on the sofa, his arm stretched across the back. "Cody, run to the kitchen and get your mother something cold to drink."

"He means *walk* to the kitchen, Cody," Merry said as Cody jumped off the floor and dashed out of the room. Lily chased after him with Charlie following on her heels, barking excitedly. Merry cut Tony a sideways glance. "You have to be careful what you say to him. He takes everything literally."

She heard the kids in the kitchen, arguing over which can of soda to choose, followed by a loud *thunk* as the soda can hit the floor.

Well, so much for that cold drink, Merry thought ruefully, hoping they didn't try to open it before giving it to her. She didn't feel like scrubbing soda off the ceiling tonight. They meant well, but it wouldn't be the first time she'd received a "geyser" can.

"Merry," Tony said, interrupting her train of thought, "I realize the final decision is yours, but—"

The disappointment threading his voice made her conscious of how selfish and uncaring she must look right now. She opened her eyes and sat up. "Please understand; I don't have an issue with the dog, it's the children I'm worried about. Aidan's arrest and all of the problems I've battled since then have affected both of them. Lily clings to me, afraid I might leave her, as her father did. She sucks her thumb when she gets upset or tired. With Cody, it's just the opposite. He's become mouthy, stubborn and rebellious."

Cody and Lily burst into the living room with the soda. Cody held out his hand. "Here's your drink, Mom!"

"Thank you." Merry smiled and gingerly accepted the can, hoping it didn't explode in her hand. "Now I need a cookie."

As they raced back into the kitchen and out of earshot again, she carefully set the unopened can on the coffee table. "As I was saying, Cody is going through a difficult phase right now where he simply doesn't listen to me. Look what he pulled today, ducking under the garage door after I told him specifically to stay in the car. I'm worried he won't take his responsibility with the dog seriously and neglect the poor little guy."

"Perhaps you could give Cody a trial period," Tony replied, "with the understanding that having the dog is a privilege and if he doesn't take that privilege seriously he'll lose it."

She shrugged. "That sounds reasonable in theory, but it puts the burden of enforcing it on me. Besides, I don't have a fence around my backyard for the dog to safely run and play. What if Cody throws a ball that bounces into the street and Charlie is hit by a car while chasing after it? Once the damage is done, there's no going back. I just don't want my kids to suffer any more heartache than they've already gone through."

Tony leaned forward. "I understand your concerns and I'm not trying to tell you how to raise your children, but I believe Cody could learn a valuable lesson in responsibility if you give him this opportunity to prove himself."

She tipped her head back, wondering what to do. He did have a point, but...

She sighed, knowing it would be unfair to Cody to deny him this chance to grow as a person.

"For one week." She gave Tony a stern look, letting him know she still held reservations about Charlie's continuity of care in her house. "Cody gets a one-week trial period, and if he doesn't show me he can be depended upon to care for Charlie and keep him safe, the dog goes back to you."

Tony let out a deep breath, looking visibly relieved. "Thank you."

Cody and Lily rushed into the living room followed by Charlie, his tail wagging, his claws clicking a short, staccato beat on the oak floor. Cody set a saucer in her lap with a grin. "Here's your cookie, Momster!"

"Cody, we need to have a talk about Charlie." She motioned him to sit again in the easy chair facing the sofa. "I've decided the dog can stay. Wait—" She held up one hand, motioning the cheering boy to sit down again. "Do you promise me you'll take good care of Charlie? He's counting on you to give him food and fresh water every day."

"Yes, Mom." Cody nodded solemnly.

"Do you promise to stay in the backyard with him when you're outside and never allow him near the street?"

Cody nodded again, his sandy curls bobbing. "I promise, Mom. I don't want Charlie to get hurt."

"Okay, then. Charlie can stay for *one* week. If, at the end of the week, you're taking good care of him, I'll decide whether he can stay until Christmas."

"Thank you, Mom!" Cody jumped out of his chair and rushed to her side to give her a hug. "I'm so happy Charlie can stay!"

"Yeah!" Tony held up his palm to exchange a high-five with the boy. "Let's celebrate." He pulled his phone out of his pocket and pulled up his contact list. After a few moments, he said, "I'd like to order a large sausage pizza to be delivered."

Merry stared at him in surprise. Pizza didn't rate high on her list of favorite foods, but it sounded wonderful tonight. She managed a small smile at the prospect of not having to cook or clean up a meal, although if she had cooked dinner for the kids, chicken noodle soup, buttered toast and apple slices would have sufficed.

"We're having pizza! Thanks, Tony!" Cody showed his happiness with a crow hop around the room.

Still on the phone, Tony leaned close to Merry and whispered, "Do you want something else? How about lasagna?"

She turned toward him. Their faces were so close. The bold

scent of his cologne filled her head, making it even more difficult to think. "Why...don't you want pizza tonight?"

"I'm more of a steak and potatoes guy, but I do like pasta occasionally."

She managed a weak smile. "As long as I don't have to cook it, I'm fine with whatever you decide."

He turned back to the phone. "I also want two orders of lasagna, a couple dinner salads with Italian dressing and an order of garlic breadsticks. How soon can you deliver it?" He recited her address and hung up.

Lily crawled onto Merry's lap and curled up. "I'm hungry, Momma."

Merry slid her arms around her youngest and stroked her hair. "The pizza will be here soon, okay? You can have my cookie."

Satisfied with that for now, Lily munched on the sugary treat. "I like you, Tony," she said, still curled up on Merry's lap. "I like you to be my friend forever."

Tony smiled, though his gaze rested on Merry's. "I'd like that, too."

Lily lifted her head. "Are you coming to the party?"

He looked puzzled. "Party?"

"Yeah, Mom," Cody said from where he sat on the floor with Charlie, "can Tony come with us to the Christmas party?"

She hadn't planned to invite him. After all, they'd only known each other for two weeks and she didn't feel comfortable asking him to come along—even if it only amounted to a family-style Christmas party at her place of employment. Now that the kids had confronted her in his presence, she had no choice.

"We're...um...going to an old-fashioned Christmas celebration

73

at the Nicollet Island Inn next Tuesday night. Do you...do you want to join us?"

He didn't answer at first, as though grappling for an excuse to refuse.

She cringed inside at his hesitation, feeling stupid for putting him on the spot.

Of course, he doesn't want to go to some boring event with me and the kids. He probably has other plans that night with someone else—a successful, educated, career-minded woman without children or baggage and much younger than me...

"If you're busy...that—that's okay," she said, waving her hands, a small gesture to keep her mind off her humiliation. "I understand. It's short notice, anyway."

"No...ah...I can go," he said slowly, but his reluctance indicated otherwise.

It shouldn't have mattered. It was just a party for the kids and after all—she had enough problems. She didn't need a man in her life, too, complicating things.

Even so, she couldn't stop the disappointment of his reluctance from seeping into her heart.

Chapter 6

December 13th

On Tuesday night, Tony pulled into Merry's driveway at six-thirty sharp to take her and the kids to the party. He grabbed his keys out of the ignition, but remained seated behind the wheel, pondering what to say to her. As he gazed at the brightly colored mini-lights bordering her kitchen window, his stomach twisted with apprehension.

He had a lot to explain.

First, he needed to come clean about his relationship to Faith and Neal Carter. He didn't expect her to be happy about his connection to them, nevertheless she deserved to know. The longer he put off telling her, the more it would look like he had something to hide—which he didn't.

Secondly, he had to acknowledge the elephant in the room—his embarrassing hesitation last Friday night when she asked him to attend the Christmas party at the Nicollet Island Inn.

It was an innocent request, *but she had no way of knowing what she'd asked of him.*

She didn't know how drastically his life had changed in a single moment or how many times he'd revisited the night Cherie and Evan died, wishing he'd gone home and picked them up instead of insisting Cherie drive separately to the Christmas party where he waited for her and his son. The decision had stolen his joy and turned the holiday season into a reminder of everything he had lost. Tonight, however, he meant to turn that corner of memory lane, put one foot in front of the other and keep going, no matter how much it hurt. He wanted to enjoy this night with Merry.

He opened the vehicle door and slid out, intending to start mending their friendship by apologizing.

The kitchen door burst open before he had a chance to knock. Cody stood before him wearing navy twill pants and a crewneck sweater with burgundy, navy and white stripes. Charlie stood faithfully at his side. Tony smiled and lightly rapped his knuckles on Cody's forehead, acting as though he couldn't stop in time.

Cody burst out laughing and reached out, attempting to get Tony back, but Tony stepped into the kitchen and danced around like a boxer in the ring, playfully blocking each blow. Charlie skirted around them and barked, happily joining the fray.

"Hey, you two, horsing around is not allowed in my kitchen!"

All *horsing around* abruptly ceased. Tony turned and saw Merry standing in the doorway in a black velvet dress accentuated with a single strand of shimmering pearls. Her long blonde hair draped her shoulders like a veil of golden silk.

"Hello," he said, sobering as his gaze met hers. "You look beautiful."

"Thank you." Her voice held a note of reserve and he knew he needed more than a compliment to convince her how much he wanted to see her tonight. He'd thought of nothing else since the last time they were together.

"Thank you for inviting me." He moved close to her. "I've been looking forward to this night since—"

"Tony!" Lily came running into the kitchen. She wore a green velvet dress trimmed in white faux fur and belted at the waist with a matching satin ribbon. She spun around for his inspection.

"Well, look at you," Tony exclaimed as he took her hand and twirled her in a circle. "All dressed up like a princess. Is that a new outfit?"

She nodded. "Grandma Lauren made it for me."

He gently tugged on her ponytail. "You're going to be the prettiest girl at the party."

Next to your mother, he thought and looked up. "Merry, I need to have a word w—"

"Look, Tony," Cody said as he knelt next to Charlie, clutching a tennis ball. "Watch *this*." Charlie sat like a statue, his liquid brown eyes focused on the ball as Cody balanced it on the bridge of the dog's nose. "Hold still, Charlie..." Cody let go. The ball rolled down the side of Charlie's snout, but the dog's reflexes were swift and he jumped, snatching it in his mouth. Cody's face beamed with pride.

"Good job, both of you," Tony said with a grin of approval. Though it made him happy to see Cody bond so quickly with the dog, his thoughts stayed centered on Merry and wishing he had a moment to talk to her alone.

Merry looked up as she helped Lily with her coat. "Shall we go? The parking lot at the Inn fills up quickly."

Tony zipped his jacket and drew his keys from his pocket. "It's already full. I drove by it on my way here and even the overflow spaces at the park pavilion were nearly gone, too."

"Cody, stop playing with the dog and get your jacket on."

Merry pulled on her knee-high boots then snatched her coat off the back of a chair. "Why don't we walk? It's a clear night and the exercise will do us good."

"All right," he replied, thinking they could talk on the way.

He took Merry's coat and held it for her. She slipped her arms into it and as he tugged the gray wool garment over her shoulders, his fingers brushed the back of her neck. He paused, captivated by the smooth, soft touch of her skin. He leaned close, tempted to kiss that beguiling little hollow spot behind her ear.

Merry suddenly drew in a deep breath and glanced over her shoulder, as if reading his mind...

Lily yanked on Merry's sleeve. "Momma, I need my present to put under the tree at the party."

Merry blinked, regaining her composure and said, "It's on the dining room table, honey. Get Cody's gift, too."

They said goodbye to Charlie, locked the back door and started out. The temperature, a crisp thirty degrees, made for a pleasant walk in the still night air. The kids were excited about the party, especially Cody, and he kept up an animated conversation all the way to the Inn.

Once they turned onto East Island Avenue, the square silhouette of the Inn, lit with multi-colored lights, came into view. By the time they reached the parking lot, thoughts of that dreadful night three years ago had blown into a major distraction in Tony's mind. A deep sadness welled up in his soul, creating a level of anxiety he hadn't experienced in a long time.

I don't want to think about it anymore, he brooded, upset with himself for allowing that same old tune of despair to play in his head. He held open the door for Merry and as she passed, his nostrils filled with the rich floral scent of her perfume. *This is where I want to be, and whom I want to be with,* he thought, fighting the urge to put his arms around her and hold her close.

The kids ran through the lobby and bounded down the stairs to the lower level where dozens of people milled about the party room, sipping on punch and munching on snacks while their children participated in a variety of games. Tony and Merry encountered a huge tree, flocked in white at the base of the stairs, glittering with glass ornaments and blue twinkle lights.

Cody and Lily placed their gifts under the tree then made a beeline for the children's craft corner.

Tony stood next to Merry with a smile pasted on his face, but deep down he struggled to keep his mind off how much he missed his son at times like this. Evan would have been seven by now and excited to come to a party like this one. He longed to see his only child sitting at the craft table, happily coloring with friends. Instead, he saw Cody and suddenly realized the God-given opportunity he'd received to bless someone else's child.

Suzanne Grange waived at Merry from across the room. She smiled at Tony when she saw him standing next to Merry and headed straight toward them with two glasses of punch.

"Hey, there, Tony," Suzanne said and handed him a glass of wassail. "How have you been? I haven't seen you since that day at Merry's place when you had your head stuck under the hood of her car."

Her sense of humor made him forget his problems. "That was me all right." He laughed. "How are you?"

"I'm working too much!" She grinned, revealing a tiny gap between her front teeth. Oddly enough, it added to her attractiveness. "I spent two whole weeks arranging this party. Glad it's almost over!" Suzanne turned to Merry, offering her the other glass. "Oh, by the way, there was only one slot left for a carriage ride so I signed you up. It's at seven forty-five." She chuckled. "You owe me."

Merry let out a sigh of relief. "Oh, thank you! The kids have talked of nothing else ever since I told them you hired our neighbor, Katie Flynn, to give rides with her father's horse and carriage. They love Grandpa Flynn's horse."

Suzanne leaned close. "Are we still on for Thursday?"

Merry's expression turn sober, causing Tony to wonder why Suzanne's question had changed her mood.

"Yeah," Merry said, "Rosella's making Swedish meatballs for dinner. She says it will be ready at five-thirty."

"That will give us ninety minutes to pick up the kids from school and..." Suzanne raised one brow. "Do our thing in the garage..."

Merry simply nodded.

Tony refrained from asking, but he wondered what she meant by *doing their thing in the garage.*

The night passed quickly. The kids spent most of the evening playing games and making Christmas crafts, assisted by several of Santa's elves. They ate buffet dinner with Tony and Merry and had an opportunity to visit with Santa. Cody made a miniature frosted gingerbread house, while Lily strung together a bracelet of red and green beads.

"Oh, my gosh," Merry said, grabbing her purse. "It's almost seven forty-five. We're going to miss our carriage ride if we don't hurry." She sprang from her chair. "If you'll get our coats, I'll round up the kids and meet you upstairs at the entrance."

Five minutes later, they boarded Katie Flynn's black leather carriage, pulled by "Johnny," her father's bay gelding. Cody begged Katie to let him and Lily sit up front on the buckboard with her. Tony and Merry had the open carriage all to themselves.

"How's Grandpa Charlie today?" Merry asked once they

boarded and spread a red plaid blanket over their laps.

Katie turned in her seat, her strawberry blonde hair tumbling past her shoulder. "He's doing better, but we're taking things day by day. I don't know when he'll be able to leave the hospital."

"Tell him Merry Christmas from us," Merry said, "and we hope he's able to come home soon."

"I will. Thank you." Katie turned around, made a clucking sound and tapped the reins lightly on Johnny's rump to set the carriage in motion. Cody chattered non-stop, asking her questions about the horse and pestering her to allow him to hold the reins.

Grateful someone else held their attention for the time being, Tony slid his arm along the backrest and leaned close to Merry, breathing in the rich tones of her fragrance. "It's so nice," he murmured in her ear, "to have a moment alone with you."

"Enjoy it while you can," she replied with a wry smile. "It won't last long."

The blanket on their laps kept them warm in the crisp night air as the carriage rambled across the narrow Merriam Street Bridge over the east channel of the river and onto the cobblestone street along St. Anthony Main. Many of the shop windows, now dark, were dressed in pine garland, red bows and brightly colored ornaments. The steady clip-clop of Johnny's hooves dancing on the pavement and the tree-lined street dotted with streetlamps replicated to resemble antique gaslights took on a serene, small town atmosphere, even though they were in the heart of Minneapolis.

The carriage ventured along the river to the end of Main Street, turning around at Lucy Wilder Morris Park then began the journey back to the Inn.

Tony snuggled his arm around Merry and pulled her close. "I'm sorry about the other night," he said softly in her ear. "I didn't mean to make you feel like you were pressuring me to come tonight with you and the kids."

She looked up, her wide brown eyes filled with hurt. "Why did you, then?"

"Because," he said, relieved to get it off his chest, "for the last two years I've done everything I could to avoid Christmas."

She sat up straight, her eyes widened with surprise. "Why?"

His gut clenched, but he cleared his throat and continued. "Three years ago, my wife and son were killed in a car accident on the way to a Christmas party." He held up one hand to silence her next question. "No, I wasn't driving. I had such a tight schedule that day, I asked Cherie to drive separately."

"Oh," her brows drew together, her face stricken, "I'm so sorry."

He looked away, not wanting her to see the guilt he knew showed on his face. "I blame myself. If I would have made the effort to go home and get them instead of insisting they meet me at the party, they would still be alive."

"It's not your fault, Tony. Accidents happen." She paused. "If I'd known how difficult it was for you, I would never have pressed you to come."

He shook his head. "There's no way you could have known. It has been difficult, but I'm finally coming to terms with losing them and I want to move on." He took her hand in his. "Ever since I met you, I've begun to realize how much of life I'm missing. I've tried to forget the past, but until now, I haven't had a good reason to let it go."

Her eyes softened with care. "What has changed?"

He looked deeply into her eyes. "The way I feel about you." His gaze lowered to the soft, moist curve of her mouth. Slipping his fingers under her chin, he tilted her face and brushed her lips against his. His heart began to race as the sweet taste of her mouth, soft and warm on such a crisp night reached into his soul, filling a huge void and giving him a sense of unity that he hadn't experienced in a long time. Wanting more, he slid his arms around her and pulled her close, deepening his kiss.

She hesitated at first, placing her hands on his chest, as if to protect herself from opening her heart to him, but as he circled his arms around her waist and drew her to him, she exhaled a deep breath and slid her hands across his shoulders, curving them around his neck.

"Mommy, I'm cold. I wanna sit with you."

The sound of Lily's voice wrenched them apart. Breathless, they turned and faced the front just as she stood up and tried to climb over the buckboard.

Katie placed one hand on Lily's shoulder. "Okay, honey, you can join your mom, but wait until the carriage stops."

Once Katie pulled the horse to a halt, Tony leaned forward and stretched out his arms, safely transferring Lily into the carriage. She climbed onto Merry's lap and snuggled under the blanket.

The carriage ride resumed. Tony realized their ride was almost over—and his chance to finish their conversation.

"Merry, I'd like to take you to dinner on Saturday night," he said, tucking the blanket around Lily's shoulders. "Just the two of us."

"I'd *love* to go, Tony, but..." She sounded uncertain, her brows knitted together with worry. "I have to work. That reminds me, I still need to find a babysitter."

Determined to spend at least some part of Saturday night with her, he made a quick decision. "I'll do it. I'll watch the kids for you."

Her eyes widened in surprise. "Thanks for the offer, but I don't want to impose on you like that. You know what a handful Cody is."

"What?" He asked incredulously. "You don't think I can handle your kids for a couple hours?"

She cocked one brow. "Are you sure you want to? I mean, you'll be passing out food and settling squabbles all night long."

He waved away the notion that he didn't measure up to the job. "It'll be a piece of cake!"

She burst out laughing. "Right. Okay, what time can you be over to my house for some *crazy* cake?" The corners of her mouth curved upward in a mischievous smirk.

"What time do you need me to be there?"

Merry shifted Lily on her lap, now sound asleep. "I have to be to work by three for the start of the dinner shift."

"No problem. I'll be there by two-thirty. Oh, and you'd better save your appetite for later. I plan to order takeout for when you get home."

"Oh, no you don't." Her eyes sparkled. "This time it's *my* treat."

Tony smiled as he tucked the blanket around Lily's shoulders. "Fine, I'll bring the wine..."

By the time they arrived back at the Inn, Tony realized they would have to wake Lily to walk home. He said to Merry, "Why don't you wait inside? Cody and I will jog back to the house and get the car."

Katie overheard their conversation and twisted in her seat. "Your little girl must be really tired. Why don't I give you all a ride home? I have to bring Johnny back to the house, anyway, to load him onto the trailer and take him back to his stable."

Merry let out a loud sigh of relief. "Oh, thank you, Katie. That would be wonderful."

"Yeah!" Cody shouted and bounced in his seat. "We get another ride!"

Katie drove the carriage up Merry's driveway and stopped at the back door. Tony climbed out first, and held Lily as Katie helped Merry climb down. Once inside the house, Charlie met them in the kitchen, his tail thumping as he greeted them. Tony brought Lily upstairs to her bedroom and laid her on the bed.

"I'll see you on Saturday afternoon," he said to Merry once they were back downstairs in the living room, "but I'll call you tomorrow. Maybe a couple times..." He slid his arm around her and kissed her goodnight. He didn't want to leave, but she had to get up early tomorrow to get the kids off to school. The rest of their talk would have to wait until Saturday night, when the kids were sleeping and he had her all to himself.

He drove home with the car radio blasting Christmas music, happier than he'd been in a long time.

****

December 15th

At four-thirty on Thursday afternoon, Merry, Suzanne and the kids arrived at Rosella Connor's home in a modest neighborhood in Northeast Minneapolis. They pulled into the driveway of the two-story stucco house and the yard light suddenly blinked on. Merry waved at her ex-mother-in-law, standing inside the three-season porch at the back of the house as the two-car garage door slowly rolled up. Rosella's green, late model Toyota sat in the center of the building, surrounded by a hodge-podge of tools, ladders, small engines and lawn and snow equipment.

Merry twisted around to talk to the kids in the back seat. "Cody and Lily, you go in the house. Suzanne and I will come in after we get Dad's boxes organized in the garage, okay?"

"Okay, Mom." Cody unbuckled his seatbelt, pushed open the passenger door behind Suzanne and jumped out.

"Wait for your sister!" Merry opened her door and slid out of the vehicle to open Lily's door and unfasten the seatbelt in her car seat. Once accomplished, she set Lily on the ground and watched the kids race to the back porch where Grandma Rosella, plump and gray-haired, stood holding the storm door open, welcoming them.

"Hi, Rosella! Suzanne and I will come in the house after we get these boxes put away."

Rosella hollered something about "putting the coffee pot on," but the kids interrupted her, grabbing her attention away as they chatted excitedly and pulled her into the house.

Merry joined Suzanne at the opened hatch of the vehicle and grabbed a box. "There's a spot in the back left corner by the wall where we can move some things around to store these." Suddenly she let out a groan, followed by an exasperated sigh. "With all the commotion going on trying to get the kids ready, I forgot that folder with the burial information for Rosella on the kitchen table!"

"Oh, well." Suzanne shrugged. "We'll remember it next time."

Merry found everything stacked in the garage exactly as she'd left it the last time she'd snooped around the place. The garage had become Aidan's personal "man cave" for car maintenance and small projects after his father passed away. Rosella only went into the building to park her car or retrieve it.

She dropped a heavy box of paperwork on the floor and flipped on the main light. "We'll put these over there," she said to Suzanne and pointed to a corner filled with lawn and garden items. "We can pile the flower pots and stuff on the work bench."

Suzanne made a slow, 360-degree turn, taking in the cluttered environment inside the building. "Wow, I can see why you put off moving all these boxes *here*."

They jumped into action, moving rakes, hoses, sprinklers, trellises and various sizes of flowerpots out of the corner so they could move the boxes into that space. Within minutes, they finished their work and closed the overhead door.

"Now," Suzanne rubbed her hands together, "let's get started with the search." She made a sweep with her left hand. "You take that side and I'll cover this one."

Merry approached Aidan's workbench and began to comb through his tools, looking behind his small storage chests of screws, nuts and bolts, digging through the drawers then pulling them all the way out to see if her ex-husband had taped a key or note in an inconspicuous place. She opened a three-pound coffee can full of loose change. The force of pulling off the lid caused some of the money to spill on the workbench and fall to the floor.

Suzanne's eyes widened at the sight of all that silver. "That will buy all your Christmas presents and then some."

Merry scooped up the coins and dropped them back into the red can. "I've been meaning to give this to Rosella. She's on a fixed income and she could use the extra cash. I just wanted to make sure Aidan hadn't hidden a key in there." She went to replace the lid and did a double take. Aidan's wedding ring poked out among some quarters. Gritting her teeth, Merry re-sealed the can and shoved it aside.

Rosella can have the ring. I never want to see it again—or anything of his.

"Is this Aidan's main tool chest?"

"That's it, but it's facing backwards." Merry stared at Suzanne across the hood of Rosella's car and watched as Suzanne tried to turn it around. "The wheels probably need oiling. You want some help?" She walked around the car and assisted her friend. Once they turned the front facing outward, she gave one of the top drawers a tug. "H-m-m-m... I must have locked it the last time I searched the garage. Darn, I should have brought Aidan's key."

Suzanne dug into her pocket. "You mean this one?"

Merry laughed. "Where did you get that? I watched you throw it back into the box at my house."

Suzanne bent down and shoved the key into the lock. "We just happened to bring that box with us so I located the key while you were helping the kids. Yikes, this lock is either really dirty or the key is bent."

She worked it back and forth until the key finally turned and they heard a faint "click" as the lock opened. Suzanne eagerly pulled open the first drawer and found it empty. She opened the second and found it bare as well.

Merry watched Suzanne open drawer after drawer—knowing they'd find each one in the same condition as the first. "See? I told you it was empty. I have no idea what Aidan did with all the tools he kept in here. This thing used to be full."

"Did you hear that?" Suzanne bent down and peered into the bottom drawer. She pulled it back and forth. "Hear that scratching sound?" She looked up. "Is there a flashlight handy?"

Merry reached across Aidan's workbench and grabbed one from a shelf. She pressed the "on" button and got no results "This one is dead. There are a couple more here, but I don't know if I'll find one that still works." She thought for a moment. "Wait a minute. We can use Aidan's trouble light. That is, if we can find it."

"Over there!" Suzanne pointed to the light hung on a long nail pounded into a stud along the open wall.

Merry grabbed it and plugged it into the electrical outlet by the service door. The LED light shone brightly as Suzanne knelt and inserted it into the drawer. "There's something stuck in the back. It feels like it's caught in the track." She reached in and tugged on the object.

Merry heard a tearing sound and almost swallowed her tongue as Suzanne pulled out three quarters of a hundred-dollar bill. They gasped in unison then stared at each other in disbelief.

"So...it's true." Suzanne turned the bill over and examined the other side. "He did convert all the money to cash. This must be where he initially stored it. The question is; where did it go from here?"

"I don't know." Merry forced back a frustrated sob in her throat. "But I'd give anything to find out."

Chapter 7

December 17th

Tony arrived at Merry's place on Saturday afternoon at two-thirty sharp with his Jeep full of tools and a detailed plan. First, he wanted the kids to have a good time in his care. That meant keeping them busy with projects. Second, he intended to surprise Merry by making necessary repairs to her kitchen and bathroom. He wanted to do something special for her, to be good to her in the best way he could. Babysitting and fixing things around the house might not seem like romantic gestures, but they came straight from his heart.

"The kids go to bed at eight-thirty. Don't let them talk you into staying up later," Merry said as she slipped her coat over her white oxford shirt and black slacks. She grabbed her bag. "They can get themselves into their pajamas and brush their teeth, so you shouldn't have to deal with that. Lily usually goes right to sleep, but Cody likes to read a while. There is a hot dish in the refrigerator and a bag of fresh green beans in the freezer. All you have to do is heat them both in the microwave. Oh, and there's a list of phone numbers on the counter in case you have an emergency."

"Hey," he murmured, buttoning her coat as an excuse to pull her close. "Relax, everything's gonna be just fine." He gave her a quick kiss, aware the kids were watching. "Have a good night."

"I should be home around ten." She smiled flirtatiously. "Save your appetite. I'm bringing a surprise!"

Tony gave her a goodbye hug. "I'm starving already..."

After Merry left, Cody opened the refrigerator and stared inside. "When are we having supper? I'm hungry."

"I think we should order a pizza." *It's the easy way out*, Tony thought, *but it doesn't involve cooking or washing dishes.*

"Yeah!" Cody danced around the kitchen with glee. "I like it when you come over!"

Lily tried to copy him by jumping like a kangaroo. She backed up and knocked a brown accordion folder off the counter. Papers spilled all over the floor. Everyone scrambled to pick them up, but the papers didn't go back into the folder as easily as they fell out.

Tony looked at the jumbled mess and sighed. "Put it somewhere safe, Cody. I'll try to straighten it out later."

They played with Cody's remote control car until the pizza arrived. After they had devoured a large pizza and a jug of soda pop, Tony gave each of the kids a gift. Lily received a huge coloring kit, complete with crayons, colored pencils, markers, water paint and several coloring books. He handed Cody a small black nylon case.

Cody gingerly peered inside his gift. "What's this?"

Tony grinned and rumpled the boy's hair. "It's a tool kit. Want to help me fix some things around the house?"

"Yeah!" Cody dug into the case, pulling out a small wrench. "That's way cool!"

Lily took over the kitchen table, painting a unicorn in her

coloring book as Cody tied on his new carpenter's apron. Tony put Cody to work right away helping him reattach the closer to the kitchen screen door. They installed weather stripping to the frame and a deadbolt lock on the main door. After that, they fixed the leak under the sink that dripped into an ice cream pail and they tightened the hinges on all of the cabinet doors. Then they took apart the ceiling light to clean it and replace all of the burned out bulbs with new, energy efficient ones.

With tail wagging and ears perked, Charlie followed Cody everywhere they went. While they worked, he stretched out on the floor and slept. Tony tried coaxing the dog away from their workspace, but Charlie always came right back and flopped down next to Cody, oblivious to the fact that he was in the way.

Merry called Tony's cell phone at seven-thirty to check on the kids. Cody insisted on talking to her.

"*Mom*! Guess what! Tony got me some *real* tools." Cody's face beamed with pride. "And guess what we're doing--we're fixing the toilet!"

Tony chuckled; he was glad Cody enjoyed their time together. Merry did a great job of raising him, but the boy needed a positive male influence in his life, too. Tony never got the chance to raise his own son, but he wanted to be there for Cody.

Tony managed to get his last project finished and pick up his tools by the time eight-thirty rolled around. He helped Lily put her colors and paints back in their case and reminded the kids of their bedtime. Lily ran upstairs to change into her pajamas and brush her teeth, but Cody folded his arms and refused to budge.

"You're not my dad," he said, his face darkening with a sullen frown. "You can't tell me what to do."

Tony stared in surprise, taken aback by the boy's abrupt change. He thought for a moment and replied, "You're right. I'm not your father, but I *am* your friend and friends don't treat each other like that,

92

do they? I'm not trying to tell you what to do; I'm simply following your mom's orders."

Cody's eyes grew wide, as though he hadn't expected such an honest response. "I don't want to go to bed. I want to stay up with you."

"I understand that, but if I don't do what your mom says, she might not allow me to come over again and stay with you when she has to work."

Cody's brows knit together as he mulled over the consequences. "Okay," he said slowly and started for the stairs. "Come on, Charlie."

The dog followed him up to bed.

Tony had just settled onto the sofa to take a breather when he heard Lily calling his name. He bounded up the stairs, worried something might be wrong. He found her in bed, tucked under the covers, hugging her favorite toy, a small stuffed lion. "What's the matter, sweetheart?"

She looked up. "We have to say a prayer."

He sat on the edge of her bed. "Um...okay."

"Like this," she responded, clasping her hands.

He put his palms together, his fingers entwined.

With her eyes shut tight, she tilted her face toward the ceiling. "Now I lay me down to sleep." She stopped and looked up at him. "*Tony*, you have to close your *eyes*."

"Oh, sorry about that," Tony said and scrunched his eyes shut.

"I pray the Lord my soul to keep. Amen."

H-m-m-m...didn't that prayer contain a couple more sentences? He refrained from commenting, deciding to let her do it her way. "Amen." He stood. "Nighty-night."

"Will you read a book to me?"

"Well..." He glanced toward the door, wondering how to get this kid to quit stalling. "You need to go to sleep."

She gave him an innocent look. "Just one? I promise then I will..."

He walked over to her bookcase and found a book lying on the top shelf. "Lama, Lama, Red Pajama," he said, reading the title.

"That's my favorite! I want that one."

He sat on the bed again and started to read aloud. Halfway through the book, he looked up and found Lily fast asleep hugging her stuffed lion, her thumb lodged firmly in her mouth. She looked so angelic and peaceful he almost wished he'd had a daughter of his own. He closed the volume and stood, placing it back on the bookcase on his way out.

"Hey, Tony," Cody summoned as Tony passed the boy's bedroom door.

Expecting more resistance, Tony stopped at Cody's doorway. The boy lay sprawled on his bed reading an astronomy picture book in his red Spiderman pajamas. Charlie lay curled up next to him. "What's up?"

Cody sat up. "I'm sorry I was mean to you," he said in a contrite voice. "Don't tell my mom, okay?"

"No problem," Tony replied, glad they were mending their differences. He walked into the room. "We'll just keep it between us."

Cody nodded, visibly relieved. Then his expression grew serious. "Are you guys going to get married?"

What? Tony almost fell over. "*Married?* W-why do you ask?"

Cody stared at him. "I saw you kiss her."

At first, he didn't know what to say, but decided to keep it simple. "We're just friends."

Cody's face took on a solemn expression, as though he'd given the situation careful thought. "Well, it's okay with me if you ever want to."

"Thanks. I'll keep that in mind." Tony smiled, warmed by the boy's acceptance of his closeness with Merry. "Hey, is that book about the solar system? I used to have one like that."

They spent a few minutes thumbing through the pages and talking about constellations until Cody began to yawn. Tony said goodnight and went downstairs, relieved to have some down time before Merry arrived. Grabbing the remote, he turned on the television and collapsed on the recliner. He tried to watch a movie, but Cody's words kept repeating in his mind. Getting married didn't register anywhere on his radar, but getting to know Merry better certainly did.

****

Merry heard faint sounds coming from the television when she entered the kitchen later that night. She set her bags on the table, pulled off her shoes and padded into the living room where she found Tony snoozing peacefully on her green corduroy recliner. A small lamp on the adjacent drum table cast a soft glow on his face.

She recalled how quiet he had been at the Christmas party. Though he didn't mention it, she'd sensed his discomfort all through the evening and she assumed he'd found the event boring. Later, when she learned of his wife's death, she realized the truth. It must have been a difficult situation for him to bear, but he'd endured it simply to be with her.

She'd never met a man like him before—so caring, so selfless. Since the day they met, he'd gone out of his way to do thoughtful, helpful things for her. They were minor tasks for him, such as fixing her car and the garage door, but his actions had resulted in major blessings for her.

Merry couldn't deny she found him tempting. Any woman in her right mind would be attracted to this tall, dark, hunk of a guy. Even so, she couldn't trust her heart to anyone—Aidan's betrayal had made her think twice about that. Why, then, wouldn't that small, still voice in her soul leave her alone? Why did it quietly keep urging her to give Tony a chance?

Tony must have sensed her presence for he suddenly awoke. "Hi," he said softly and ran his hands through his hair. "I guess I dozed off."

She smiled. "It takes a lot of energy to keep up with my kids."

"They were actually very good." He yawned and sat up. "I just kept them busy."

Merry unbuttoned her coat and hung it in the closet. "Did they give you any trouble at bedtime?"

"Ah...no." He stood, shoving his hands into the pockets of his jeans. "Everything was cool."

Her stomach growled. "I'll hurry and check on the kids so we can eat before our dinner gets cold. I'm starving."

"What did you get?"

"It's a surprise!" she replied in a stage whisper and ran upstairs. Stopping at Cody's door, she poked her head into his room. He'd fallen asleep with the dog and a half-dozen books lying on his bed. She stacked the books on his desk, gave Charlie a pat on the head and turned out the light.

Lily slept peacefully in her bed, sucking her thumb as she held on to her stuffed lion. Merry kissed her forehead, gently pulled Lily's thumb out of her mouth then partially closed the door and went back downstairs.

Tony stood in the kitchen, opening a bottle of wine. "I didn't peek, I swear."

In the living room, Merry set a brown shopping bag on the coffee table along with candlesticks, plates, silverware and napkins. Tony followed her with two wine glasses in one hand and a bottle of white wine in the other. They sat together on the sofa.

"Sweet and sour pork, sesame chicken, fried rice," she said as she pulled out the cartons, "egg rolls and fortune cookies from The Dragon House."

"Smells great." He grinned. "I haven't had Chinese food...for a week."

"Quit teasing," she said with a laugh and pretended to slug his shoulder.

"This food hits the spot," Tony said as they ate dinner. "The Dragon House is one of my favorite restaurants. Speaking of which, how was your night?"

"We were crazy busy and I'm beat!" Merry picked up her wine glass. "The good news is I made enough money in gratuities to pay my heat bill, fill my gas tank *and* buy groceries." They touched the rims of their glasses together. She studied his features, intrigued by how his thick, tousled hair and five-o-clock shadow gave him a ruggedly handsome look by candlelight. "Thank you so much for watching the kids. You have no idea how much I appreciate it *and* all of the things you fixed around the house tonight."

"I wanted to do more, but I ran out of time." He sounded sincere, but his eyes reflected the same cloud of unease she saw at the party. He had something pressing on his mind.

"Enough about me. We're always talking about me," she said and speared a slice of egg roll with her fork. "I want to know more about you."

The question must have hit a sensitive spot because he stilled, his hand frozen on his wine glass as his eyes searched hers. After a moment, he said, "I have a confession to make."

I knew it. He's in love with another woman. He likes me as a friend, but... Her breath caught in her throat. Her heart tightened in her chest. *I should have known better than to think a man as sexy and desirable as him would be available much less be interested in me.*

The silence grew into an uncomfortable pall over the room. Her fork stayed in mid-air, forgotten while she waited for him to spill the truth.

"Everything I've told you about me is true," he said quietly. "It's what I haven't told you that's the problem." His jaw tensed. He stared intently into her eyes. "You see, I'm more than just a random investor who bought the contract on your house."

Her palms began to sweat. What did he mean by that?

"I know the couple responsible for sending your husband to prison," he continued, "his employers, Neal and Faith Carter. Faith is my sister."

Oh. My. Gosh...

Her head began to swim, but she kept herself steady out of sheer will. She set her fork down, the food no longer appealing. Once she found her voice she said, "What do you want from me, Tony? Or is that even your real name?"

"All I want is your friendship, Merry. I swear I didn't intentionally mislead you." He pushed his plate away and leaned toward her. "I'll admit I was skeptical of your ability to keep your payments current when I purchased the contract. Once I met you, everything changed."

She glared at him, still needing answers. "If you had doubts about my credit worthiness, why did you buy my contract from the

Granges in the first place?"

"It was a business deal. Like I said, I'm an investor and my name *is* Anthony Lewis. I own dozens of contracts-for-deed. You can easily find me on the Internet."

"Why did you wait so long to tell me this?"

"I didn't want to say anything in front of your children, especially Cody. I didn't think you'd want him to overhear this conversation." He tossed his napkin on the coffee table. "This is the first time I've had you truly all to myself. You know that. I'd planned to tell you the night of the party, but I never got the chance. So I decided to wait until tonight."

She exhaled an anxious sigh and moved away from him, still staring daggers at him. "Is there anything *else* you haven't told me?"

"Yeah," he said boldly. "There has always been only one woman who's held my heart in her hands and I'll never find another like her, but she's gone and it's time to let her go. There's someone else in my thoughts now. Someone who is very special to me." His searing gaze stunned her as he clasped his hands around hers and pulled her face close to his. "The first time I saw you, something about you tugged at my heart. Every time we're together, that pull gets stronger and I can't get you out of my mind. You make me feel alive again, Merry. You give me more reasons to be happy than I can count. I'm sorry it took me so long to tell you about my connection to the Carters. I don't want any secrets between us. Ever again."

He drew her into his embrace and kissed her deeply, sending her pulse racing. As his arms tightened around her waist, she let go of her fear and slid her palms up his chest. Her arms circled his neck, pulling him closer. The spicy aroma of his cologne lingered on his collar, filling her nostrils with his masculine scent. No one had *ever* kissed her like this. No one had ever *energized* her like this. She loved his gentleness, his strength, his passion. Kissing him made *her* feel desirable again and she didn't want him to stop.

She kissed him again and again, caught up in a rush of euphoria. Her heart soared at the thought of not being alone anymore, not having to depend solely upon herself anymore. But her hopes dashed when suddenly Aidan's betrayal flashed through her mind, dredging up her desperate two-year struggle to emerge from both an emotional and a financial crisis.

Panic overshadowed her and she pulled back. "I can't...I can't do this."

He gazed into her eyes. "What's wrong?"

"It's not because of you, Tony. I want to, but after what Aidan did to me and the kids, I can't risk subjecting my family to such heartbreak again. It will be a long time before I'll trust anyone in that way."

Pressing his lips against her ear, he murmured, "Look, I'm not Aidan. I would *never* hurt you like he did." He pulled back and lifted her chin. "Can't you see the way I feel about you is turning my life upside down, too? I know what it's like to have my heart broken, but I'm willing to take the risk."

Emotionally drained and exhausted, she looked away, trying to make sense of her jumbled thoughts.

He gently put his arms around her again. "We'll take it slow. I promise."

They were silent for a long time, holding each other.

Tony eventually spoke. "Are you still hungry? We didn't finish our dinner."

Merry nodded as she pulled away and picked up her plate. Ravenously hungry, she devoured it all, not caring that it had turned cold.

They finished eating and brought the dishes to the kitchen. Merry opened the pantry door to find a container for the leftovers when something fell out and crashed to the floor. Looking down, she saw the contents of the accordion file for Rosella Connor scattered across the kitchen. She rolled her eyes. "Oh, no."

"I'm sorry about the mess," Tony blurted as he swooped down and began gathering up the pages.

"No, no, it's my fault. I should have caught it before it hit the ground."

"Cody knocked it off the counter right after you left." Tony grabbed a fistful of paper. "I hope it's not important information."

She scooped up the remaining sheets and dumped them on the kitchen table. "It's actually not mine." She sat down and attempted to put the pile in order. "I'm giving the entire folder to Aidan's mother. It's the burial information for his father and two of his aunts. Aidan handled all of the arrangements. I'd better organize the pages and clip them together so they never come apart again."

"Here's another one," Tony said as he picked a sheet off the floor.

Merry began to quickly sort through the pages, making a pile for each deceased relative. She picked up a wrinkled sheet and frowned. "This is odd."

Tony glanced over her shoulder. "What's that?"

"It's a ten-thousand dollar receipt for a custom, double upright monument. I don't know how I missed this, but maybe I didn't pay any attention to it because it's from the same company that makes all of the family gravestones." She glanced at the date then scrutinized the document, noticing someone had stapled it to at least one other sheet, but the additional pieces were missing. "Aidan ordered it two months before his arrest. According to this, the monument is black granite with companion stones and urns, and our names are engraved on it." She looked up. "I know nothing about this purchase. How dare he buy such an expensive monument without telling *me*?"

Tony shrugged. "Maybe after handling everyone else's funeral in the family, he decided to start getting his own affairs in order."

"That's no excuse," she replied as she continued to scrutinize the receipt. "He had it installed at Angel of Mercy Cemetery in Humbert Falls, where his father is buried." She smacked the receipt on the table. "That place is in the middle of nowhere, surrounded by cornfields. I don't want to be buried there, least of all, next to him!"

Tony slid his palm along the nape of her neck. "Calm down, tiger. It's not worth getting upset over. The damage has already been done."

"I'm working doubles to give my kids a decent Christmas because my ex stole every penny we had. And now I find out he squandered thousands of dollars of *our* money on a stupid memorial to himself!" She folded her arms and let out a tense breath. "I have Monday off. The kids are on Christmas break and spending the day with Grandma Connor so I can get some shopping done, but I just might drive up to Humbert Falls instead and check it out." She shot him a wry grin. "Maybe I can re-sell the monument on Craig's list next spring. Get some of my money back."

Tony laughed. "I doubt that."

"I still want to drive up there and see it."

He shot her an incredulous look. "Are you serious?"

"Yes," she said and began sorting papers again. "I just found out I have a gravestone with my name on it. How creepy is that? I think I should investigate it."

"You shouldn't go alone. Want some company?"

She shook the folder and a couple paper clips fell out onto the table. "Angel of Mercy is two hours north of here and it's a boring drive. There's nothing but frozen prairie all the way."

"I'm never bored when I'm with you." He picked up a large clip and handed it to her. "I love being with you."

His answer made her pulse jump. "I love being with you, too."

He smiled, but his eyes reflected seriousness. "I'll pick you up on Monday morning at eight."

Chapter 8

December 19th

On Monday morning, under a gray, overcast sky, Tony pulled into Merry's driveway at eight o'clock. He shut off the Jeep and stared at her kitchen window.

She works so hard, he thought, watching her dash back and forth. *She should be enjoying the season with her kids instead of pulling double shifts and trying to catch up in between.*

He resented Aidan Connor for causing her present situation. How could a man rob his own wife—and children—leaving them destitute? Connor's narcissist, self-centered greed had caused Merry a lot of heartache, but the man would never get the chance to hurt her again. Not if he had anything to say about it.

He slid out of the Jeep and walked to the house. She met him at the back door in a pair of black leggings and a long, fuzzy pink sweater. Her shining blonde hair hung in a fancy braid over one shoulder.

"Hmmm..." He drew in a deep breath. "You've been baking again."

She smiled. "I made frosted cinnamon rolls and a fresh pot of coffee. Come in and have one while they're still warm."

He circled his arm around her waist and pulled her to his side, giving her a kiss. "Hey, you're spoiling me."

Merry began to laugh, her eyes sparkling. "You've already spoiled me!"

Twenty minutes later, Tony had the GPS programmed on his phone and they were on the road to Humbert Falls. He had no idea what they would find, but it didn't matter; he wanted to support Merry in any way he could. If that meant driving her somewhere up in the boondocks to check out a cemetery on a gloomy December day then so be it. He wanted to gain her trust, something that loser Aidan Connor had destroyed.

"Tony," Merry said once they were on the freeway, heading out of town, "I need to ask you something but I don't want you to take it the wrong way."

The wariness in her voice made his hands grip the steering wheel. Whenever a woman prefaced a question with a condition, she expected a certain answer. At least, Cherie always did...

He drew in a tense breath and pretended to concentrate on the road. "Go ahead," he said and signaled to move into the left lane.

She shifted in her seat, facing him. "On Saturday night you said 'only one woman held your heart in her hands and you'll never find another one like her.' Does that mean you'll never love anyone but her?"

Her question startled him. He glanced at the side mirror and changed lanes to buy time to think carefully about his answer. "No," he said slowly, "it means she's one of a kind and what we had will never be duplicated. It doesn't mean I can't love someone else or that I even want the same kind of relationship again."

"What was she like?"

He sensed her studying him. "Cherie had a Master's Degree in English and she taught classes at the University. She loved teaching and did a lot of volunteer work, tutoring kids with special needs. When Evan came along, she put her career on hold to be a full-time mom. She'd planned to homeschool our son."

Too much information, Lewis, he chided himself. *You're making your late wife sound like a saint.* He grabbed his travel mug and took a sip of hot coffee, but in his haste, he tipped the mug too far and burned his tongue.

Merry went silent for a few moments then folded her arms. "Gosh, how can anyone measure up to the memory of someone so perfect?"

"No one is perfect, Merry," he said, attempting to pull his foot out of his mouth. "No relationship is perfect, either. It's just the way you remember someone when they're gone because that ideal image is all you have left." He grabbed her hand and gently squeezed it. "Let's not talk about the past anymore, okay? We have each other and that's all that matters today."

"Okay, but...what about your relatives? How do you think they would react to the ex-wife of the thief who embezzled your sister's money?"

You knew you had to address that eventually...

"My family is an opinionated bunch, but they're good people. They trust my judgment." Tony let out a disgusted snort. "That is, except my brother-in-law. Neal's attitude drives me up a wall, but I put up with 'Butt-Head' for Faith's sake." Tony began to laugh. "He'll probably choke on his beer when he finds out about us. What irony, huh?"

Merry looked at him as though he'd gone crazy, but soon joined in with a small giggle. Before long, they were both laughing so hard, Tony could barely see to drive.

You'd better tell her... It's now or never.

"I need to fill you in on something."

Her jubilant mood immediately sobered. "I thought we'd agreed there would be no more secrets between us."

"This isn't really a secret," he said, attempting to downplay the issue. "It's more like a technicality." He swallowed hard. "Ah...Charlie isn't my dog. I invented the boarding issue so you wouldn't have to pay me for fixing your car."

She stared at him. "Who does he belong to, your obnoxious brother-in-law?"

"He belongs to Cody and Lily."

"What?" She sounded confused. "You're not making sense."

"I bought Charlie at a shelter for the kids because Lily told me her dad gave her dog away and I could see it made her sad," he said and dug his hand into the bag of cinnamon rolls. "I plan to give Charlie to them for Christmas." He started to take a bite of his roll then stopped, casting a sideways glance in her direction. "I hope you don't mind."

"Of course I mind," she spouted and rolled her eyes, feigning disapproval. "You're in big trouble, buddy—giving my kids a dog without asking me first."

"For the record...I'm asking you now."

She smacked her lips together. "Yeah, except it's a little late. Cody and the dog are inseparable. You couldn't take Charlie back now if you wanted to."

"You're right," he said with a mouthful of sugary frosting. "That's the point."

She surprised him with a kiss on his cheek. "Thank you. That's the nicest gift anyone has ever given my children."

He leaned toward her with sugary lips to kiss her back and didn't notice the car had veered to the right until the driver next to them laid on his horn. *Oops...*

They drove in silence for a while then turned on the radio to listen to Christmas music. Before long, the urban landscape of shopping centers and housing developments gave way to snow-covered fields and the occasional steeple of a small town church. Merry spent the remainder of the trip taking a well-deserved nap. Tony turned the radio down low and relaxed as he drove. He knew she needed the rest. She didn't awaken until he'd turned off the freeway.

"Where are we?" Merry yawned and stretched in her seat.

"Just coming up on Humbert Falls," Tony replied. He checked his phone. Once they passed through town, they still had a ways to go.

A mile past the town, he turned off the blacktop onto a bumpy, snow-packed gravel road. The tools for repairing his duplexes shifted in the back of his Jeep as he turned the corner, reminding him to slow down. He followed the road until he saw a white church with a bell tower. Behind it, he saw a small cemetery divided into two equal sections by a one-lane road. The area hadn't received much snow so far and most of the graves were visible.

Tony drove up the driveway, past the church to a small parking area next to the building and shut off the Jeep. "I'll follow you," he said as he pulled on his cap and gloves.

Merry led him straight to the Connor family plot. "Here are the newest graves, Aidan's great aunts, Ida and Olga Johnson," she said, pointing to a pair of shiny flat headstones in pinkish-gray granite among a row of similar ones. "They were twins—spinsters—who died a month apart." She turned to her left and pointed to a gray, upright monument. "Dougal Connor, Aidan's father is right there." She looked around. "So...where is *my* monument?" Her lips turned up in a mischievous smile as she held out her palms. "The one fit for a queen?"

"You tell me," Tony said, scanning the area. "Are you sure your ex actually had it installed? Maybe he had the order written up but never went through with it."

"I saw the paid stamp on the receipt," she said as she scanned the vicinity. "This area is full. Maybe Aidan couldn't get two plots together next to his family's graves. Let's look around."

They wandered through rows and rows of headstones, all sizes, shapes and colors as they made their way across the cemetery. They found the gravestone in a back row on the opposite side, surrounded by other large monuments.

The tall, shiny structure sat on a wide cement foundation, flanked on each side with a matching square stone and a granite vase. Tony stared at Merry's name on the stone. "How does it feel to stand in front of your own grave?"

"It's creepy." Merry shivered as she stood in front of the massive ink-black display of polished granite.

Tony knelt next to one of the "companion" stones and examined the large bronze medallion located in the center. Using a key to pry it up, he noted the hidden hinge needed oiling. "Merry, look at this." He pointed to a combination lock with four numeral dials.

Her jaw dropped. "What is it? A safe?"

"I think it's a time capsule," he said as he rolled the dials to see if they needed oiling, too.

Her face paled. "Do you think Aidan might have stored—"

"It's possible, but we can't get into it without the combination." Tony sprang to his feet. "Let's go back to the Jeep and warm up first." He glanced at the sky. "It's getting colder and the clouds are turning so dark I think it might start snowing soon."

They hurried back to the Jeep and started the engine while they drank the last of their coffee and discussed possible combinations.

"We could try to guess the combination and hope we get lucky," Tony said as he stared through the windshield at the monument, "but unless Aidan used an easy sequence, there's little chance we'll crack it. He doesn't strike me as the kind of person who'd go to all this trouble to hide his money and not have a tough set of numbers to protect it. On the other hand, we could try to break it open."

Merry looked intrigued. "How would we do that?"

He thought for a moment, wondering if he had the right tools. "I might be able to force it open with a hammer and a crowbar, but it'll destroy the time capsule and damage the stone."

"At this point, I don't care." Merry shrugged. "I don't plan to use it, anyway. I just want to know what's down there. If the first one is empty, we won't need to bother with the second one."

He shut off the vehicle and jumped out. "Let's get a move on."

Tony found what he needed in the back of the Jeep. At the monument, he placed the crow bar on the lock and raised the hammer. "Are you sure you want me to do this? Even if it is your headstone, what I'm about to do amounts to vandalism." He glanced around nervously. The church blocked their view of the road, but that didn't mean they were in the clear. He didn't want to have to explain his actions to the Humbert Falls police if someone driving by heard the noise and reported them.

She stared at him, her jaw stubbornly set. "Yes, do it!"

It took three strikes as hard as he could hit. Chunks of black granite flew with each slam of the hammer, the sound echoing through the air with the intensity of a bomb blast.

"Wow," Merry exclaimed once he busted a hole in the lock. "You did it!"

He used the crowbar to force it open the rest of the way. Peering into the opening, he said, "I see something in there." He shoved a bare hand into the capsule and pulled out a bundle of hundred dollar bills.

Merry gasped and stared at the money as though she couldn't believe her eyes. "Tony, is there more?"

He stood and gestured toward the stone. "It's a square chamber in the ground and from what I can tell, it's full. Go ahead, see for yourself."

Merry's slender hand easily slipped into the capsule and pulled out three bundles. "We found it! We found the money!" Laughing hysterically, she sprang to her feet and threw her arms around him.

It did his heart good to see her so happy because now she could prove her innocence, but the open capsule exposing all that money gave him a sense of urgency. "I'll find something in the Jeep to transport it."

At the Jeep, he saw a car in the distance and hurried back to the grave. "Start filling this gym bag with the bundles while I tackle the other lock," he told Merry when he returned. The second capsule, however, didn't break open as quickly as the first one had. His hands shook from nervousness and the necessity to hurry, making it difficult to wield the hammer.

"I have to hand it to your ex." Tony picked a bundle out of the second capsule and fanned the bills. "Storing the money this way is a *very* clever move. Connor must have suspected his employers were on to him so he came up with this idea to keep it safe. It would have remained here until he got out of prison if we hadn't come across the receipt." He leaned over and tossed the money into the bag. "What I want to know is—what happened to the money you jointly owned?"

Merry dragged the large gym bag over to the second capsule

and began to transfer the second half of the bundles. "Ten thousand of it probably paid for the monument. Between the equity in the house and our investment accounts, I figure he made off with roughly four hundred thousand, so yeah, I'd like to know what he did with it, too."

"Maybe some of it is mixed in with this," Tony said as he held the bag open. You don't know the exact dollar amount of his embezzlement, do you?"

"No, but I think I should let the Carters' insurance company determine if I overpaid them." She paused. "What I want most is to clear my name of all suspicion of wrong doing and restore my reputation. I'll call the Minneapolis police as soon as we get home and turn the money over to them."

The snow began to fall, a few flakes at first, but within a couple minutes, they could hardly see what they were doing. He and Merry emptied the second capsule as fast as they could, but the snow began to fall swiftly, hampering their efforts.

"We look like Olaf, the snowman in Lily's coloring books," he said as he and Merry struggled to zip the overstuffed bag.

She stared at his hand. "What happened to your thumb?"

His jaw clenched. "Stupid hammer..." He needed a drink to kill the pain, but didn't have time to think about that now. In this weather, just getting home would take all of his concentration.

Tony stood and shook the snow off the brim of his cap then hoisted the heavy bag over his shoulder. Working out several times a week had finally paid off. "Let's go."

Suddenly Merry let out a startled cry and gripped his arm. Turning around, he froze. Neal and another man he'd never seen before were marching straight toward them.

****

Merry recognized the tall, stocky man with salt-and-pepper hair as Neal Carter. A shorter man, slight of build with thinning reddish hair brought up the rear. They both wore plain, dark clothing. She had no idea how they'd found this place, but it didn't take a genius to figure out why they were here.

Tony slid his arm around her, his muscles tensing as he pulled her close. "What are you doing here, Neal? I don't recall inviting you."

Neal hungrily eyed the gym bag with a satisfied smirk. "I came to pick up my money."

His money? Since when?

Merry slid from Tony's grasp and sprang forward. "It's not your money! We're turning it over to the police. Leave us alone or I'll call them right now."

"Go ahead, get 'em out here," Neal said arrogantly and pointed toward the damaged monument. "I'd like to see you explain *this*."

Tony scowled. "She didn't hide the money and she doesn't have to defend her actions to anyone, including you."

"She's as guilty as that criminal she married." Neal glanced at his sidekick then turned back to Tony. "Hand over the money, Lewis, or we'll take it from you."

Merry slid sideways, creating a barrier between the men. "Stop this!"

Neal pushed her out of the way. She stumbled backwards, her phone slipping from her pocket into the snow. She picked it up. "I'm calling 9-1-1 and reporting you!"

"Go ahead." Neal said with a derisive snarl in his voice. "Who would believe *you*?"

Calling his bluff, she dialed 9-1-1, keeping watch on the developing scene while she talked to the operator.

Tony shoved the bag off his shoulder, his hands clenching as it dropped to the ground with a thud.

After seeing him destroy the time capsule, Merry knew he had the strength to put his brother-in-law out of commission for a long time. Tony helped her to her feet then he went after Neal. She winced, expecting him to slam Neal in the gut, but instead he grabbed the man by the front of his jacket, his voice shaking. "You touch her again and so help me, you'll wish you hadn't!"

Neal wrenched Tony's hands from his jacket. "Don't threaten me." Then he nodded to his partner. "Marv…"

The weasel of a man pulled back the right side of his coat, placing his hand on a holstered revolver.

"I'm not leaving until I get what I came for," Neal said.

Unfazed, Tony began pacing back and forth with fists clenched, glowering at the seedy-looking guy with the gun. "I hope what he's paying you is worth the risk of losing your P. I. license." Tony shook his fist at Neal. "You're not going to get away with this!"

Merry ended her call and stood next to Tony.

"Come on, Neal," Marv said and attempted to lift the gym bag. "We need to get out of here."

Merry stared at the men as unanswered questions bombarded her thoughts.

How did they know where to find us? No one knew we were driving to Humbert Falls. Unless…

She planted herself squarely in Neal's path. "How did you know we were here?"

"We followed you." He gave her a smug look. "I always knew you had the money hidden somewhere, and all I had to do was bide my time until you showed *him* where to find it."

Something didn't add up here. Her mind began to race. The only way Neal could have *known* to follow them would be if he knew Tony had befriended her...

She folded her arms and stepped in front of Tony, nearly colliding with him. "You told him about us, didn't you? What else are you keeping from me?"

Tony stopped pacing and stared at her as if she'd gone crazy. "I didn't tell him anything, Merry, I swear."

"I wouldn't bet the farm on that," Neal said in a braggart voice, obviously enjoying the friction between them. "The little lady wants you to fess up, Lewis. Didn't you tell her why you bought the contract on her house?" He laughed. "I had to pull a fast one on you to get you to do it!"

Neal's derisive laughter stung. Her heart began to slam in her chest. "Tony, is that true? He coerced you into buying my contract?"

"Don't listen to him, Merry." Tony clasped her hands, his eyes pleading. "He's just trying to cause trouble between us by twisting the facts."

Uncertain, she pulled away.

"He balked, didn't like the terms," Neal continued, "but I know how to get what I want. Don't I, Lewis? All I have to do is dredge up what Faith did for your dead wife and I've got your undivided attention."

What a jerk.

Merry couldn't tolerate Neal Carter much longer, but if Tony had lied to her, she needed to find out. She leaned against a tall monument for support. "So you needed his help. Tell me why."

"Someone had to get the information out of you," Neal said and strained to pick up the gym bag. "We had a deal—a ten percent finder's fee."

Tony's face paled. "No, we didn't!"

Neal dropped the bulging bag and gasped for breath. "Are you denying the meeting at Sam's Bar never happened?"

"We met but when I found out what you wanted, I turned you down flat!" Tony lurched forward and grabbed Neal by the throat. "Look, I've had enough of your lies, you dirty—"

"Back *off...*" Gun-toting Marv pulled the pistol from his holster and thrust it into the center of Tony's chest. Tony shoved Neal away, glowering with disgust.

"Check with Gerald Grange if you don't believe me," Neal said to Merry as he drew in a deep breath. "I met with him, bargained for a good price and brought in Lewis." Neal gestured toward Tony. "He orchestrated the whole thing."

Tony's eyes blazed. "I didn't orchestrate anything. I considered it a *business deal*, nothing more!" He turned to Merry. "He wanted me to spy on you, but I refused to help him. I stuck up for you because I believe in you. Merry, I care for you. I'm on your side!"

With startling, heartbreaking clarity, things began to fall into place. Though Tony denied his involvement with Neal, the evidence mounted against him. He had asked many pointed questions the first time they met. He also took note of every detail in her house. Her heart sunk with the realization that he'd used every excuse he could muster—the car, the dog, the kids, the sob story about his wife—as a ruse to pull her into his confidence, locate the money and earn the fee.

She should have suspected something when he insisted on driving her to Humbert Falls. All that talk about not liking Neal might have been true, but he obviously was willing to put up with the creep for the money. He even had the proper tools at the cemetery. How many men would just happen to have a three-pound hammer and a crowbar in the back of their vehicle? The ugly truth hit her like a punch to the gut. *He'd been working with Neal all along.*

Now Neal was double-crossing him and he had to lie even more to save face...

Nausea formed in the pit of her stomach as the pain of betrayal gripped her heart. Like déjà vu, a familiar onslaught of rejection, disillusion and hurt washed over her. But this time, things were different because the disaster with Aidan had slowly changed her, made her stronger somehow. This time she wouldn't fall apart. No matter how much she ached inside, she wouldn't allow herself to become a victim. This time she'd control her own destiny.

The wail of a police vehicle sounded in the distance.

"Get that thing out of my face," she snapped at Marv and pushed his pistol away. She pointed her index finger at him, but had a good mind to use another. "I'm not afraid of you."

She turned on Neal next. "That goes for you, too, mister. You *disgust* me. Take the money. And get out of my sight." Neal and Marv each picked up one end of the bag and headed for their car, shuffling through the snow.

In the distance, a police siren grew louder. She couldn't see it through the falling snow, but knew it wouldn't be long before the squad car arrived. If they chose to run, they wouldn't get far.

"And you..." She glared at Tony through tear-filled eyes. "I should have known better than to trust you. You *used* me."

"Merry, you've got this all wrong." He gripped his hands on her shoulders and looked into her eyes. "Please, listen to me. I swear, I didn't—"

"Yes, you did. You knew about this, all of it," she spat and slapped his hands away, barely able to keep her emotions intact. "Yet, you chose to keep it from me. You insisted we not keep secrets from each other, even though all the while you had plenty of secrets yourself. You're a liar and a hypocrite. How could I ever trust you again?"

"I'm sorry. I didn't mention Neal's involvement with Gerald Grange because it had nothing to do with my decision to buy the contract and I didn't want to take the chance that it would come between us." His eyes filled with sadness and it broke her heart even more. He'd royally screwed up and he knew it. He'd crossed a line, made a mistake he could never undo.

She turned away, not wanting to show how much he'd broken her heart. "I have nothing more to say."

Tony stood in her path, forcing her to look at him. He stared deeply into her eyes, struggling with regret. "You need to get back home. I'll take you."

"I'm going with the police. Don't worry about me. Goodbye, Tony." She turned her back on him and walked away as the tears tumbled down her face.

Chapter 9

December 21st

Only three cars remained in the rear parking area at the Nicollet Island Inn. No way could she miss him. He held out a slim hope he could talk some sense into her, but since she wouldn't return his calls, it seemed unlikely.

Tony parked his Jeep in the main lot and approached Merry's car. He checked his phone, noting she'd be coming out the back door any minute now to go and pick up the kids from school.

The kids...

Oh, how he missed them.

Oh, how he missed *her*.

The back door opened. A kitchen worker, clad in solid white, came out and threw a garbage bag into the metal trash receptacle then disappeared into the building.

Tony leaned against her car and waited. Looking around, he wondered if her Cavalier needed attention and fought the temptation to look under the hood. Someone needed to check the oil and examine the battery cables regularly to make sure they were tight. That someone used to be him, but not anymore. He sighed, his heart heavy with a profound sense of loss.

I should have leveled with her. I should have told her everything. She deserved to know about Neal's proposition, but I wanted to spare her feelings. I wanted to protect her from being hurt again...

He sighed, unhappy with himself for not letting it go. After all, he'd finally let Cherie go. Her memory no longer had any power over him.

If I've lost Merry for good, I'll get over this, too.

The door opened again and Merry walked out wearing her gray wool coat. At first, she looked down, concentrating on keeping her footing on the icy ground. When she looked up, their gazes met and she faltered. Though her face didn't show emotion, her eyes reflected all the anger and pain he'd caused her. He didn't move, waiting for her to react first.

She slowly walked toward him. "Why are you here? Are you stalking me?"

He stayed leaning casually against the front fender with his arms folded, his ankles crossed, but his heart thumped so hard it sounded like kettle drums beating in his ears. "You haven't returned my calls. I can't even leave a message."

"We've said all there is to say."

Her pallid skin and the dark circles under her eyes attested to the strain the last few days had caused her. It wrenched his heart to see her looking so tired; it bothered him even more to know he had been the cause. He wanted to take her in his arms and comfort her. Promise her the world, and give it to her. Tell her how much he—

She stopped just shy of the front bumper. "I have to get going."

He pushed himself away from the car to let her pass. "Neal turned the money over to the police. They were waiting for him when he got home. The police turned it over to the insurance company."

"Good." She nodded curtly.

"The incident got reported on the ten o'clock news. Now everyone knows you're innocent."

She reached into her purse and pulled out her car keys. "I suppose you collected your finder's fee."

"There wasn't any fee. Neal made that up to tempt me." His jaw tightened. "Even if I'd gone along with his plans, I wouldn't have accepted it. My loyalty isn't for sale."

She opened the car door and slid inside. Tony stood next to the car with his hand resting on the open door. "Merry, I'm sorry. I never meant to hurt you. I—"

"Don't, please..." She went very still and looked down, as though fighting to control her emotions. The thought of her starting to cry caused a hard lump to form in his throat. Suddenly she shoved the key into the ignition and started the car.

There were no more words to say, no more chances to change her mind. He opened his jacket and pulled out an envelope. "This is for you," he said and handed it to her.

Merry accepted it with a nod and shoved it into her purse. Without another word, she shut the door.

Tony watched her drive away, hoping she would one day find the happiness she deserved.

Chapter 10

December 24th

"More coffee?" Merry held the pot of freshly brewed French roast above Suzanne's cup.

Suzanne deftly took the glass pot from her hand. "Sit down, Merry. I can serve myself." She refilled both cups and put it back on the coffeemaker. "You look tired. How are you holding up?"

"I'm fine, really. I've just been working too many shifts." It sounded like a plausible excuse, but she knew Suzanne didn't buy it.

Joyful laughter echoed from the living room where Lily and Cody watched the movie "Home Alone" on television.

At least the kids are enjoying Christmas Eve.

Before her confrontation with Tony at the Inn, her anger had kept her going. She'd found it easy to operate in that mode and get a lot done at the same time. Since then, however, her mood had dropped to a new low—and her productivity. She had gifts to wrap this morning, a shower to take and a salad to make for dinner at her parents' house, but she could hardly get off the chair.

If only he hadn't said, "Merry, I'm sorry. I never meant to hurt you."

He'd sounded sincere, contrite even, but his betrayal had hurt her so deeply no words could ever make things right. Not the way they used to be, anyway.

Suzanne, dressed to the nines for Christmas Eve in green velvet and gold jewelry, helped herself to a plate of homemade sugar cookies. "I wish things would have worked out. You were so right for each other." She dipped the star-shaped treat into her coffee. "Is there any chance I can get you two back together?"

Merry let out an exhausted chuckle. "No, Suzanne, and don't get any ideas because I'm over it. I'm over *him*, okay?"

Suzanne stared at her long and hard. "Are you sure?"

"Positive." She sipped her coffee and sniffed, trying to appear indifferent. Suzanne's stare made her feel like a suspect undergoing an intense interrogation.

"You still have to make payments to him every month."

Suzanne's scrutiny began to annoy her. "Maybe not. He may have sold the contract to someone else." Merry reached for her purse, remembering the envelope Tony had given her the other day. She ripped it open and pulled out a sheet of paper, staring at it with confusion. This couldn't be right.

"What is it?"

Merry looked up. "I don't understand..."

Suzanne snatched it away and scanned the document. "According to this, he's paid it off." She looked up. "You own the house free and clear."

Merry's heart began to thump wildly. "Why would he do that?" She grabbed the envelope to put it back and found a smaller one inside.

Tearing it open, she discovered a plain white card in Tony's scrawling handwriting.

Now you have the freedom to work less and spend more time with your children. Take care, Merry. I wish you all the best in life.

Tony

She began to hyperventilate. Placing her hands over her heart, she gasped for breath as her eyes overflowed with tears. The memory of their last time together flashed through her head. His love had shone in his eyes, but at the time, her anger had blinded her to the truth. "I didn't know..." The words sounded like a high-pitched squeak.

"Yes, you did. That's why it hurts so much. You should have never let him go. He's a good man and he's good for you." Suzanne shook her head with a sigh. "Maybe he did get caught in the middle of a mess and screwed up by not telling you about Neal Carter's scheme, but he's human. And he loves you. The question is; what are you going to do about it?"

"Nothing, it's over between us." Merry burst into tears, sobbing like a child.

Suzanne scooted her chair close, sliding her arm around Merry's shoulders. "Sweetie, I love you dearly, but if you don't go after that man, *I will*. He's one in a million." Handing Merry a napkin to wipe her eyes, she said, "I'll watch the kids. You're going to do this in person."

Suzanne helped her with her coat and nearly shoved her out the door. Merry started up her frozen car and drove to Tony's house. Right away, her nerves jangled.

This might be for nothing. I don't even know if he's home. If he is, maybe he won't talk to me.

She walked up the front steps of his two-story colonial and opened the screen door. The main door stood slightly ajar. Inside, raucous cheering from a football game echoed through the house. Gingerly, she pushed it open, stepping inside a room of chocolate leather sofas, dark accent tables and a split-boulder fireplace.

She found Tony in his spacious kitchen. Wearing snug-fitting jeans and a white T-shirt, he stood at the granite-topped center island, drinking a bottle of beer. He saw her standing in the doorway and froze.

Once again, tears rushed to her eyes and she knew her face looked like a tomato, but she didn't care. Instead of struggling to talk, she pulled the small white card out of her pocket.

His eyes widened with shock. "I never thought I'd see you again."

Shrugging off her purse and coat, she let them fall behind her and ran to him, flinging her arms around his neck. The white card fluttered to the floor. "After the way I treated you, I didn't know if you'd want to."

"Oh, Merry, all I *want* is to tell you how much *I love you...*"

His mouth crushed hers as he held her tight. She closed her eyes and let go of her apprehension, breathing in the aroma of his after-shave lotion and tasting the bold flavor of craft beer. He picked her off the tile floor and spun her in a circle. She laughed, so happy to be with him again—holding her, desiring her, keeping her safe.

"I love you, Tony." She began to laugh and cry at the same time as she looked deep into his eyes. "I always have, but I wouldn't admit it to myself because I didn't know if you could love a woman like me. My life is such a mess."

"No more than mine is." He set her down, but held her close. "Merry, I've been in love with you since the day we met. I didn't realize it at first, but every time I got near you, my stomach would flip somersaults." He chuckled, making a low sound in her ear. "That night in the carriage, I finally figured it out."

"Why didn't you tell me?"

"I wanted the moment to be special for you, with wine by candlelight," he said, framing her face with his hands. "Just the two of us."

"Every moment with you is special," she said and lifted one brow. "But the wine and candlelight sounds even better."

He pulled her close, resting his cheek against hers. "We have the rest of our lives to make up for the years we've lost from hard times. I promise you, from now on, I'll do everything in my power to make you the happiest woman on earth."

"You already have." She kissed him again as a surge of joy bubbled up inside her. She had everything she'd ever wanted—love, family and a merry little Christmas.

~   ~   The End   ~   ~

(Don't quit reading yet! Turn the page and get a sneak peek of my newest Christmas story *Once Upon a Christmas*!)

Thank you for reading A MERRY LITTLE CHRISTMAS. I love writing Christmas stories because it's my favorite holiday of the year. The setting for this book, Nicollet Island, is a real place, located on the Mississippi River, which runs through the center of Minneapolis. It's not large (about 48 acres), but it contains a small residential neighborhood, a high school, the Nicollet Island Inn and a large park that takes up a huge portion of the island. The entire island is listed on The National Register of Historic Places.

The dog in this story, the Jack Russell terrier named Charlie, is a real dog and he belonged to my father for many years. Charlie has passed away but his memory lives on as the sweet little doggie in this book.

If you enjoyed this story, feel free to let others know by recommending it and by leaving a review at the retailer where you purchased it. If you'd like to know more about me or my other books, you can visit my website at: www.deniseannettedevine.com

Want a preview of some of my best books? Read the first chapters on my blog at:

https://deniseannette.blogspot.com

Sign up for my newsletter at: http://eepurl.com/csOJZL and receive a free romantic suspense novella

Like my Facebook page at:

https://www.facebook.com/deniseannettedevine

HEA – join my private group exclusively for sweet romance:

https://www.facebook.com/groups/HEAstories/

More Books by Denise Devine

Christmas Stories
Merry Christmas, Darling
A Christmas to Remember
A Merry Little Christmas

Once Upon a Christmas

Bride Books
The Encore Bride
Lisa – Beach Brides Series
Ava – Perfect Match Series

Other Books
This Time Forever - an inspirational romance
Hot Shot – a free novella
Romance and Mystery Under the Northern Lights – anthology of short stories
Recipes of Love (Cookbook)

Boxed Sets
Love, Christmas

Once Upon a Christmas

When old friends reunite, will a new enemy keep them apart?

Ashton Wyatt has spent a decade running from her past.

Hanging out with a bad crowd in high school cost Ashton her reputation, her boyfriend and her relationship with her parents. Determined to start over, she has moved far away, but can't escape the loneliness that shrouds her heart. When she receives an offer to return to the small, tourist town of West Loon Bay to revive The Ramblin' Rose Bar with her sister and her cousin, she accepts the challenge, hoping to repair the bond with her family as well. But just when her life is on the mend, she crosses paths with someone from her past and things spin out of control...

The last thing Sawyer Daniels needs is to get mixed up with the town's wild child.

Sawyer did his share of partying and keeping the local cops busy in his misspent youth, but he has long since abandoned that crowd in an effort to make some sense of his life. He's already under contract to renovate The Ramblin' Rose when he learns Ashton Wyatt is back in town. Though the situation gets off to a rocky start, their friendship grows as they work side by side. He doesn't realize how much he's grown to care for her until a stalker puts her life in danger. Now that he's finally found his true love, is he about to lose her?

Want more? Read the first chapter of this story on my blog at:

https://deniseannette.blogspot.com

94089180R00072

Made in the USA
Lexington, KY
24 July 2018